HUM

THE NEW NORMAL : BOOK 1

DAN HAWLEY

HUM
Dan Hawley

Editor: Susan Gaigher
Cover: germancreative

Copyright © 2021 Dan Hawley

For Adrienne.

HUM

CHAPTER 1

"ARE YOU EXCITED?" JASON ASKED AS HE LOOKED over at Sam.

"I am," she responded.

Her dark eyes met his from the passenger seat. "It'll be nice to get off the road." Sam's hand reached for Jason's lap as she turned her gaze out the window and towards the city. "That was a long drive."

"Drive?" Jason grinned. "All you did was sit there and be cute." Sam shot him a feigned look of annoyance. He pretended to be shocked. "But you do it so effortlessly, babe." He winked and flashed the dimples. She couldn't resist those dimples. She couldn't resist Jason.

When they met three years prior, it was like two worlds colliding. Fireworks and lighting and all the cliché love analogies. Neither of them believed it could happen until it did. Love at first sight. It was the type of thing that people on the outside look at and judge. "How could they fall in love so quickly?" people would ask sarcastically, rolling their eyes. "*That* was fast." But Sam and Jason didn't care. They could not ignore the deep stirring within them.

"Did we actually just move to the other side of the country?" Sam asked.

"Yeah we did," Jason replied. "Crazy."

"It doesn't feel real," Sam whispered.

The move made sense to Samantha on many levels, and she had considered everything thoroughly before finally agreeing. Jason had a better, higher-paying job waiting, and no doubt she would find something quickly too. More money was always good, but Samantha was also ready for adventure, for change. The city was a great choice, beautifully nestled among some of the world's most gorgeous landscapes. Seattle had almost everything they needed.

"I miss them already," Samantha said.

She was close to her parents. They had always been there for her, and she knew it hurt them deeply when she broke the news. But they understood. Her father immigrated from Japan when he was a teenager, so he knew about travel and adventure and craving something new. Her mother, though, was a homebody. Her family had lived in that small, North Eastern town for generations. Still, she could understand the draw of something different.

"Yeah…I'm sorry, babe. That's the only thing that sucks. We don't know anyone out here," Jason responded.

He knew he would miss his family and friends as well, but he was convinced this was the right move. "Like we said, though. Nothing is stopping us from packing up and moving back if we don't like it here."

"Yes," Samantha agreed. "We need to experience life and all it has to offer while we're still relatively young, right?" she chuckled. "That is, until you knock me up, and we're forced to put our dreams and ambitions aside to take care of the kids. I'll get all old and fat and tired looking, and you'll cheat on me with your young, sexy secretary."

"They're called executive assistants now, Sam," Jason chirped as he smiled.

"OK!? Don't deny it or anything!" Samantha protested, but she knew Jason would never cheat. Every relationship had its challenges, though, and theirs was no different. Even though Sam and Jason fell madly and deeply in love from the very beginning, they still had disagreements. Jason often spoke before thinking, and Sam could become offended quickly. They could both be very stubborn as well, which meant fights lasted longer than they needed to. But one thing was sure in both their minds, unwavering and true; they were deeply in love.

"And we're going to visit soon," Sam declared.

"That's true," Jason agreed. "We'll fly back in a few months for a visit once we settle in. He paused. "You're good, right?"

"Stop asking that." Samantha rolled her eyes. "You know I wouldn't have come if I didn't want to."

"I know, just checking in," Jason said. "I think this is our building."

As he eyed the tall building up ahead, he thought about how this all came to be. Late the previous year, Jason was approached by a Seattle-based software company that asked him to fly out to check out their operations. He obliged, and Samantha went along. By the time the trip was over, Jason had an attractive job offer and Samantha had a good idea about what neighborhoods she liked. The couple had truly made up their minds by the time the plane took off to take them back home. The only real negative they could see was leaving their friends and family behind. But better jobs, more money, a warmer climate, and the thrill of adventure was too much to pass up. After all, they agreed, they could go home any time if they wanted to.

As they pulled into a spot in front of the building, Samantha remarked, "It's weird that we're moving to an apartment that we've never seen."

"We have pictures and videos and had a virtual tour."

Jason unclipped his seatbelt.

"You know what I mean," Samantha said as she examined the height of the building. "We don't know how it... *feels*."

"Well, you said you liked the neighborhood and the pictures and video of the place. You liked the furniture, and the building management was professional and friendly and got great reviews online. It's also why we only signed a six-month lease. So we can test things out. Make sure we like it out here," Jason explained and added, "But yeah, it's weird."

Samantha and Jason had sold most of their furniture before the move. They'd decided it would be best to rent a furnished apartment instead of hauling everything across the country. Offloading most of their stuff would also allow them to easily move back home if they discovered they weren't settling in. Selling most of their things didn't take long, and when they packed up before they left, the couple agreed that it was odd to be able to fit their whole lives into the SUV.

After a quick stretch, the couple entered the building and found the office, where they met Chester.

"Good to see you folks." Chester smiled warmly and rose from his desk.

He was a large man but had an energy about him that made people feel at ease, like a warm cup of cocoa on a cold winter night. He was older, with greying hair and a thick beard. He had the sort of belly that comes with age and a love of food. But beneath the layer of fat, Jason could tell that Chester had thick muscles and was once in phenomenal shape. He extended a hand that was bigger than Jason's entire face.

"How was the drive?"

"It was good," Jason replied, making sure to clasp Chester's huge hand as best he could and offer a strong, manly shake. "It was a bit boring until we hit the mountains. Man, they are something else, huh?"

Still smiling, Chester nodded.

"They sure are. Ok, I've got your keys here, and I'll take you up after I show you your parking spot down below."

Chester grabbed the keys in his large paws and started towards the door. Samantha and Jason looked at each other with excitement and followed.

It didn't take long to bring everything in from the parking garage to the apartment on the 21st floor. The front door opened into a short hallway with a mirrored closet on the right for shoes and jackets. The white tiles then transitioned into hardwood flooring as one moved further into the apartment. On the left was the kitchen, which opened to the living room. Dividing the two spaces was a granite-topped island meant for eating, with two stools tucked alongside.

The kitchen was stocked with all the essentials: dinnerware, pots and pans, and cooking utensils. The stainless-steel appliances and white cupboards gave the space a modern look against the dark stone backsplash.

The living room was large and bright, with a fantastic

view of the harbor from the leather couch. A recliner and giant flat-screen television rounded out the area.

The first room off the living area was going to be their office. It was big enough for a desk, a chair, and a bookshelf.

Next was the bathroom; light and bright with a deep bathtub and lots of storage for Samantha's products under the sink. A small laundry nook was hidden behind another small door.

Finally, the master bedroom was in the north-western corner of the apartment. A small wood nightstand sat on either side of a carved wood queen-sized bed. Even though Samantha said the walk-in closet was the best thing about the bedroom, Jason thought it was the view. To the west, the small, white-crested peaks of salty waves danced and fell away on the ocean's dark surface. To the north, beyond the city, stood stalwart mountains capped with snow.

"This view is insane."

"Yes, it is." Samantha agreed.

But she wasn't looking out the window. She was staring at Jason, who was sitting on the edge of the bed, staring west at the horizon. It was getting late. The earth had recently spun the last piece of the sun below its horizon, and the sky was on fire with long brushstrokes of intense color. Violent reds and crisp oranges mingled in the air, fighting an endless battle with the impending black of night approaching from the east.

Jason's silhouette popped against that background, and Samantha could see the definition in his arm and chest muscles through his tight white t-shirt. She stood captivated by the magnificence of it all. Jason looked up to see his lover eyeing him seductively.

"Oh, you meant me, huh?" He blushed a bit.

She had that look in her eyes, and he knew what that meant. His blue eyes watched as Samantha reached down, grabbed the hem of her shirt, and removed it from her body, revealing her ample breasts. She stood a moment so she could enjoy Jason's gaze on her body.

Anticipation filled the room, like fully inflated lungs holding, pausing, before their exhale.

Jason's eyes eventually made it back to hers, and she moved to stand in front of him, their eyes locked. Sam leaned over, her pouty red lips stopping less than an inch from his. They consumed each other's breath while she removed his shirt from his chiseled body. Jason reached down and caressed Sam's legs under her long, flowing skirt. Slowly, he traced up each leg before sliding her panties down. Not able to take it anymore, Samantha attacked her prey.

* * *

"I suppose we should keep putting our stuff away," Sam said as they lay locked in each other's arms.

"Or, we could just keep lying here," Jason replied. Their bodies glistened with sweat in the moonlight.

"True." Samantha snuggled into Jason's side.

"Except…" Jason said as he sat up in bed, "is that the fridge?"

"Is what the fridge?" Samantha asked.

"I don't know. That sound? Can you hear it? It's like a buzz. Is it coming from the fridge or what?"

Jason rolled over, threw his feet over the side of the bed, stood up, and slid on his boxers. Scratching his head, he headed for the kitchen.

"I don't hear anything," Samantha sighed as she rolled over to pick up her phone from the nightstand. Everyone she knew had been asleep for hours, so there wasn't much to see on social media. She started playing a song from her "Moving across the country" playlist and got out of bed. The moonlight caressed her naked body with its cold, pale light as she posed in front of the full-length mirror beside the closet.

"I definitely put on a few pounds on that road trip," she muttered.

"What's that, babe?" Jason called out from the other room.

"Nothing," Sam replied as she slid on her robe. "I was just saying the moonlight makes me look pale. I need a tan." Sam tied her robe loosely as she entered the living room. "What are you doing?"

Jason had his head cocked to one side as if exerting himself to hear better. He made his way from the fridge to the laundry, then back to the kitchen. He checked the bathroom and office and then into the bedroom to stand by the bed. Jason reached down and grabbed Sam's phone to silence the music.

"Hey, I'm listening to that," Sam started, clearly annoyed.

"Shhh," Jason sounded as he held a finger to his lips.

"Did you just shush me?" Sam's eyes widened.

Unapologetically, Jason shot her a sharp look and hissed, "Babe come on. Give me a minute."

His head cocked one way and then the other as he looked around the room, confused and angry. "Can you not hear that?" he pressed.

Samantha paused and listened. At first, she heard only silence. But then, "Oh yeah. I do hear that. Like a faint buzzing sound. It's not a big deal, is it?"

Jason crept towards the bedroom door and stopped in the doorway. He looked up the right side, across the top, and down the left. Slowly, he pivoted and lay his ear gently against the wall. Behind the paint and drywall, Jason found the source of the sound. A vibration, constant and dull, setting his nerves on edge.

"Son of a bitch," he exclaimed. "It's coming from the wall."

"I can barely notice it," Samantha sighed as she took her earphones from the dresser and popped one in each ear. "Just ignore it."

"Ugh," Jason sputtered. "It sounds like power lines. Or like one of those friggin' green transformers that buzz outside buildings."

He made a disgusted face and stuck his tongue out as Samantha turned on her phone to listen to music and unpack.

CHAPTER 2

THE NEXT MORNING, JASON'S EYES OPENED TO THE smell of fried meat and the sound of sizzling and popping in the next room. His stomach growled. Groggily he pulled himself from the sheets and made his way towards the kitchen.

"Smells good, babe," Jason commented as his mouth watered in anticipation. "Where did you get the grub?"

Samantha looked up and smiled.

"You were out like a light, so I googled the nearest grocery store, and it turned out there is a cute market just around the corner. I just grabbed a few things, but we will need a big shop later."

"Hell yeah!" Jason exclaimed. "You're the best. Need me to do anything?"

"I got this," Sam replied.

Jason pulled out a stool and sat down. Stretching his arms up and out, he said, "I didn't sleep very well, I don't think. It took me a while to get to sleep with that damn noise. I finally put in earphones. Seems to be quieter this morning though."

Samantha shrugged, plated the meat and eggs, and slid the plate in front of her man.

"Turkey bacon, huh?"

Jason poked at the thin stripes of meat with his fork. Samantha rolled her eyes.

A loud ding from the toaster oven signaled the bread had become toast. She pulled the toast from the hot oven, threw the pieces onto a plate, and began to butter them.

"Maybe you're just stressed about the move and everything. It'll get better," she said reassuringly, wiping her hands on a dishtowel. She folded a lock of Jason's hair back and gave him a little kiss on the cheek before sitting down beside him at the island.

"Well, after breakfast, I'm going to ask Chester if there is anything he can do about it."

Jason grabbed a piece of freshly buttered toast and dipped it in the pale-yellow yolk of his eggs.

"I think the office opens at 10 on Sundays."

The lobby of the building was bright, with floor to ceiling windows at the entrance. The sun's glare from the freshly buffed stone tile partially blinded Jason as he nodded to the concierge sitting at his desk.

"Good morning sir," the smiling concierge said as Jason passed. The cream furniture of the seating area looked stiff and uninviting. Jason wondered if anyone ever sat there. He opened the door to the office and went inside. The office had a classic "old man library" feel to it, with walls of books and a handmade wood desk near the back. Behind the ornate desk, Chester sat engrossed in his reading.

"Good morning Chester," Jason offered, in a tone that he meant to sound apologetic for interrupting the large man.

Chester looked up from the papers, startled.

Apparently he hadn't realized that someone entered the room.

"Oh, hello, Jason. How are you settling in?" Chester asked as he shuffled his papers back into a pile and into their folder.

"Pretty good." Jason nodded. "The view is incredible up there, and everything looks like it did in the pictures, so we're pleased with that. It's just..."

Chester raised an eyebrow.

"Please, sit if you'd like," he said, gesturing to the armchair in front of his desk. Jason hesitated. He didn't want to complain. Chester was very nice and looked busy, and Jason didn't want to take up too much of his time.

"Well," Jason began as he slid into the seat of the big, comfortable chair. "There seems to be a hum..."

"A hum?" Chester asked.

"Yes. A hum coming from the walls?" Jason more asked than stated. "It sounds crazy, but when I put my ear up to the wall, I can hear it sort of... buzzing." Jason's statement left his face looking confused, as if he was questioning his own words.

Chester's lips formed a tiny, playful smile under his beard.

"You were listening to the walls?" he asked in a lightly mocking tone.

"I mean," Jason stammered. "I was lying in bed, and I heard this buzzing sound—I thought it was the fridge, so I got up because it was so loud, but then I realized it wasn't the fridge. It was in the wall."

A moment passed, and the two men held each other's gaze. The smile on Chester's face faded, and his expression grew serious. The sudden change in the room's atmosphere made Jason shift uncomfortably in his chair.

"Do you mind if I come up and have a listen?" Chester asked.

"Of course," Jason said, thankful to move.

The elevator was silent as the two men rode up to the apartment. The gentle dings of each floor passing were like a metronome, timing their ascent. The elevator dinged one last time and stopped.

"I should have texted Sam to make sure she isn't up here naked," Jason stated awkwardly and instantly regretted it. Chester didn't seem to be in a joking mood. As Jason opened the door to the apartment, he called, "Hey babe? Chester is here. Are you decent?"

"Good morning, Chester."

Samantha was sitting on the couch wearing black tights and a white t-shirt. She put down her phone on the coffee table and stood up.

"Is Jason bothering you?" she asked.

"Of course not, dear." Chester smiled warmly. "I am happy to be of service."

Jason waited a moment for Chester to remove his shoes and head towards the bedroom. Chester paused and stood in the doorway of the bedroom. After a moment, he pressed his ear against the wall and listened.

"Hmmm."

"Do you hear it?" Jason asked quickly.

"One of the building's mechanical rooms is below your apartment. It's quite loud inside that room, but I didn't think you could hear it outside," Chester replied.

"Oh. Well, what about the people that just moved out? Did they ever complain about the noise?" Jason asked as he scratched his stubble.

Chester looked thoughtful.

"Not that I remember, no. I guess I didn't talk to them much at all, actually. But there was…" Chester trailed off.

"Was what?" Samantha asked.

"Well," Chester started. "There were noise complaints against them fairly regularly near the end. I had to come up here a few times to ask them to keep it down. The police even came once or twice."

"Big partiers, huh?" Jason mused.

"Fighting," Chester said somberly. "When they moved in, they seemed like a nice couple. I believe she was a nurse, and he was some fancy chef at one of the hotels downtown here. But the screaming! Near the end, I thought they were going to kill each other!"

Chester noticed the shocked look on Samantha's face. He attempted to provide some levity by following up with, "But they didn't, of course. They asked if they could break their lease early, and we obliged. I doubt they would have spoken since they moved out. They really seemed to hate each other." Shrugging, Chester continued, "I will go down and have a look; make sure everything is in order in the electrical room. I could call in an electrician to make sure everything is up to code and see if they can do anything about the noise. Best I can do for now." Chester smiled and turned towards the door.

He put on his shoes, opened the door, paused, and looked back at the couple.

"You two aren't like them at all. You look so in love. I can tell these things, you know." He smiled again and closed the door behind him, leaving Samantha and Jason staring blankly at each other.

Thump!

"What the hell was that!?" Samantha exclaimed after a loud noise from the window made them both jump.

"I dunno. Maybe a bird or something hit the window," a somewhat stunned Jason replied.

They hurried over to the large living room window to find nothing but a smudge.

"Poor bastard. I bet that hurt."

Samantha looked away with a sad look on her face. "Remind me never to clean the windows." She sniffed.

Moving to the couch, she looked up at Jason and said, "More and more people are dying in China every day now from that virus. It looks pretty bad on the news." She sounded concerned. Jason sat down next to her on the couch and put his arm around her shoulder. "Yeah, well, they can keep it. Damn wet markets. They must know that shit is no good!" he said with anger and a touch of fear in his voice.

Jason scooped the remote from the coffee table in front of him and pressed the power button. The screen lit up, and the 24-hour news station appeared. They were playing an endless video loop of Chinese people being torn from their homes by men in riot gear and gas masks, makeshift hospitals, giant trucks spraying God-knows-what in the streets, and mass graves. It was a grim sight. The Chinese had the city of millions of people on lockdown, and the borders of the province were closed. Still, experts and reporters discussed the potential for this new coronavirus strain to spread to other areas.

"We're ok, babe," Jason said reassuringly. "Most of the experts are saying that China has it contained, and even if it does get out, it's really just another kind of flu. It kills a lot of older people, I guess, but most people can fight it off."

Samantha nodded.

"So you're screwed, is what you're saying?" she joked as she grabbed the remote and turned off the tv.

"Oh, come on!" Jason complained. "I'm not *that* much older than you."

Samantha grinned and leaned over to whisper in his ear, "Old enough to be my daddy…"

"Oh shit!" Jason exclaimed as they both laughed. "Love you."

"Love you too."

"So, what would you like to do today, cutie?" Jason asked, grateful for the levity.

Samantha's eyes grew wide. "Explore the city!" she demanded.

And so they did.

CHAPTER 3

T HE BUSY STREETS WERE LOUD AS THE COUPLE MADE
their way outside.

"Everyone and their mother out today," Jason
complained.

The dull roar of conversations mixed with the growling of engines created an unsettling ambiance.

"It's kind of exciting, isn't it?" Sam said with bright eyes and a wide smile as she grabbed Jason's hand. Jason smiled back. "It's cool, yeah. Lots going on."

He sped up to keep pace with his lover.

"At least it's not freezing. Where is this market you went to?" he asked.

"Just up here!" Sam exclaimed, skipping towards her destination. "It's pretty cool!"

The Urban Market was a repurposed old shoe factory needed no longer in the age of globalization and sweatshops. It still smelled faintly of tanning chemicals and leather. The space was perfect for a small market. The industrial feel of concrete and brick combined with the high ceiling contrasted sharply against the vendors' colorful stands. The market comprised of perhaps a dozen vendors selling all the necessities. Samantha and Jason looked over the fruit and vegetable stands and walked past the baker. A friendly couple was sitting behind a table selling honey made from beehives located on top of a downtown building. A popular Sunday destination, people milled about in organized chaos.

"Let's just get some stuff for dinner now and go to the supermarket tomorrow after you get home from work?" Samantha asked.

"Yeah, that sounds good," Jason replied. "Maybe we can grab a bite too, while we're out."

The couple bought some fresh bread, vegetables, a few apples, and some cheese, and then made their way over to the fish vendor. While standing in line, Jason filled his lungs with the briny air.

"The fish here are way different than back home, huh?" he remarked.

Bubbling tanks full of live fish and shellfish formed a cascading glass wall. Jason saw lobster, Dungeness Crab, oysters, clams, and scallops. There were snappers, trout, and salmon— so many options.

Samantha leaned in to look at the snappers. Their black eyes set in their pink heads stared back blankly. Their little mouths were sucking and blowing water to filter air through their gills. Suddenly, a gloved hand thrust into the tank and grabbed the snapper Sam was watching. The helpless fish, expelled from the water and into the drowning air, was laid flat on a white cutting board.

WHACK, WHACK, WHACK!

Sam jumped back with alarm as the gloved hand beat the life out of the defenseless snapper with a club.

"Jesus!" she squeaked and averted her eyes.

"I was not expecting that," Jason said, his eyes wide. He shook it off and put his arm around Sam. "It doesn't get much fresher than that!" he joked with a goofy smile.

Samantha was not impressed.

"Awe, come on, babe. You know that for us to live, something has to die."

"I know," Sam whimpered. "But I don't feel bad for turnips."

Jason collected the now dead and wrapped snapper from the vendor, paid, and turned to go.

"I'll probably be a vegetarian soon," Sam remarked. "You already don't eat beef or pork, isn't that good enough?" Jason responded.

"I dunno, I just feel bad, and I don't even like it really, so why eat it?"

"Yeah, I get it if you don't like it," Jason said as they continued walking through the market.

"These days you can get away with not eating meat, since there are so many options. You have access to all kinds of different foods now that we didn't a hundred years ago. You can even supplement with powders and pills. But if all that stopped, you'd be eating my venison," Jason quipped with a wink and a dimple.

"Ugh, I'm not eating Bambi, Jay! Stop trying!" "Whatever, babe, I'm just saying, you gotta know how to survive if you need to, and if you had to, you'd eat Bambi."

Every autumn since Jason was six, he would spend two weeks deer hunting with his dad, grandpa, and a few others at a camp in northern Pennsylvania. The first time Jason shot a deer, he hit it right through the lungs—the perfect shot. The deer couldn't run for long, and the bullet didn't damage any meat.

"Great shot!" his Grandpa John declared as they both jumped up to give chase.

It wasn't long before they came upon the doe lying on the ground, struggling for breath. Its eyes were wide with terror as it looked up at Jason. Jason's eyes traveled down its neck to find the steaming hole where the 30/30 had entered its fragile hide. His 14-year-old brain was trying to comprehend what was happening; what he had just done.

Jason's grandfather could see the pained expression on his grandson's face. He put his rifle down and knelt beside Jason and the dying deer. "For us to live, Jason, something must die."

The doe gurgled and strained her final breath, then struggled no more. A few tears ran from Jason's eyes. John took Jason gently by the arm so that the emotional boy was facing his grandfather.

"Son, I understand why you feel this way. Hell, I was the same way when I took my first deer. But you do understand, Jason, this deer has provided us with food now. So there is purpose. There is a reason. Never kill without reason, Jason, you understand?" Jason's eyes dried as he nodded towards his grandpa.

"Good," John said as he released his grandson. "We will thank the deer for giving its life so that we can live longer. Its life, and death, had purpose."

With that, John plunged his hunting knife into the belly of the deer, and with surgical precision, relieved it of its guts.

* * *

"Maybe next weekend we can check out the mountains," Sam mused as she dropped the seasoned snapper into the smoking hot frying pan. The oil erupted, spitting and hissing like a snake. "Sounds good; we can put those winter tires to better use." Jason thought for a moment.

"We could go skiing if you want," he added.

Jason sat at the island, watching as Samantha expertly moved around the kitchen. With the grace of a dancer, she rolled the fish in the pan, grabbed the boiling pot of vegetables, and spun around to strain them in the sink. Salt and pepper sprinkled from her fingers onto the food in a cloud of flavor. Butter and herbs went into the pan with a splash of lemon and white wine, finishing the fish.

On to the plate it went.

With a flurry of motion, the vegetables and baked potato joined it.

Sam slid the plate under Jason's eager nose. The smell wafted up, and his mouth began to water. "You are amazing!" he exclaimed. "How did I get so lucky?"

Sam poured them both a glass of chardonnay and took a seat beside him.

* * *

With their bellies full and their dishes clean, Sam and Jason headed for the couch. Jason clicked on the tv as his feet came to rest on the wooden coffee table.

"Thousands more infected and many more dead as the coronavirus grips China. Weeks ago, the Chinese government had shut down the borders of the affected province. Still, the virus has escaped, and tonight, we are reporting the first confirmed case of COVID-19 here in the U.S.," the reporter said.

Sam looked at Jason with concern in her eyes.

"That's not good," he said, but then noticed her concern.

"We are young and healthy, babe. If we get it, it'll be ok."

"Everyone online is scared," Sam said. "They think it's the next plague. Going to wipe out millions." Jason moved to put his arm around her.

"It's not the plague, Sam. It's a bad flu that kills people who are old and have underlying health conditions. Besides, we have no idea what is actually happening in China; their government doesn't have a great track record of telling the whole truth."

Sam nodded slowly as her eyes remained fixed on the tv screen. Jason continued, "All we can do is stay healthy and remain positive. And if worse comes to worst, I always have Francine."

"You brought your shotgun!?" Samantha exclaimed in anger and disbelief. She shrugged off his arm and twisted to face him directly.

"You said you weren't going to bring any of your guns to the city. What the hell, Jay!?"

"Easy, babe," Jason replied in a hushed tone. "It was a last-minute decision. I just figured with everything going on with this virus and moving across the country to a new place where we know no one…we might want some protection."

"Protection," Samantha repeated as she rolled her dark eyes with contempt.

"Yes, protection! Listen, if this virus goes crazy and the zombie apocalypse happens, you'll be so grateful that I brought it."

"Where is it even?" Sam asked.

"I've got it locked in the office closet. Safe and sound. Nothing to worry about, babe, it's just in case. Alright?"

Sam huffed and got up.

"Don't say alright as if I have any say in the matter." She turned to walk away.

"Where are you going?" Jason asked.

"To shower."

"Well, can I come?"

"Why don't you go shower with Francine?"

* * *

Samantha opened her eyes. She lay still for a moment, then reached over to touch her phone's screen. 2:36 a.m. She rolled over onto her back and recoiled swiftly. Beside her in bed was Jason, sitting up, completely still.

"Jay?" she whispered. "Are you up?"

Jason sat motionless, staring straight ahead. Sam put her hand on his back.

"Jason?"

This wasn't the first time she had experienced Jason's odd sleep behavior. He sometimes talked in his sleep, and occasionally it would turn quite angry. Samantha even caught an elbow once when Jason was seemingly fending off an imaginary attack. Usually, though, he would mumble on for a bit and then stop. A jerky elbow or knee was rare. Even rarer, maybe twice before, Samantha awoke to find her partner sitting up in bed—just sitting there. She had tried to talk to him, but he never answered, and after a few minutes, he would lie back down, and that would be it. The next morning, when asked, he would say he didn't remember it.

Samantha withdrew her hand from Jason's back and waited and watched for him to lie back down like he had those other times. She lay there on her back, observing her lover.

His breath was like a metronome, slowly keeping time in the night air, his features bathed in the moonlight. His frame rose and fell with his breath.

Up and down. In and out. Constantly.

Samantha was almost hypnotized by the movement. Her eyes grew heavy, and sleep knocked at her door.

Then Jason's head turned quickly, and Sam could see his eyes opened wide. A look of terror was across his face. "Do you hear!?" he snarled. His breath had turned to panting, his eyes piercing hers.

"What!?" Sam yelped as she tried to escape through the mattress.

"What are you…" Samantha started, but then the expression on Jason's face relaxed and softened. He withdrew, lay down, and rolled over on his side, facing away from his startled lover. His breath became a metronome again; peaceful and constant. Shaken and rattled, Sam could do nothing but stare at his back until sleep finally consumed her.

* * *

Samantha awoke to sunlight and mint as Jason kissed her lips. The memory of last night flooded back into her mind as she pushed him away abruptly.

"What's wrong?" Jason asked, feigning hurt.

"Are you mad I have to leave you for work?" Samantha sat up in bed, rubbed her eyes, and yawned.

"You don't remember?" she asked.

"Remember what?" he searched her eyes. "Ah, was I talking in my sleep again? Must be the stress. What was I blabbering on about this time?"

"You weren't talking," Sam said. "Well, you talked, but wow, ok. I woke up in the middle of the night, and you were just sitting there. And ok, you've done that before and just lay back down, but this time was *different*." She was starting to become agitated.

"Different how?" Jason asked.

"Well, I lay there and waited for you to lie down and go back to sleep, or continue sleeping…or whatever! But instead, you turned and looked right at me, and you were so scary, you looked at me and you asked me if I had heard!"

Now distraught, Samantha began to cry.

"Whoa, whoa, easy. I asked if you heard?"

Jason sat down beside Sam on the bed and put his arm around her, rubbing her back.

"You said, 'Do you hear?'"

"What does that mean?" Jason wondered aloud.

"I don't know! You said it, and you looked so, I don't know, different, like, scared! It was horrible!"

"Then what?" Jason prodded.

"I don't know! You just rolled over and went to sleep. Then I just lay there all freaked out for hours!" Samantha sobbed and leaned in so Jason could hug her. As he put his other arm around her, he said, "I'm sorry, babe. I have no idea what that was about. I don't remember that at all, but it must have been a bad dream I was acting out or something, like before."

Sam looked up at him.

"I guess. I don't know," she said as she nuzzled into his chest. They stayed like that for a few minutes until Jason broke the silence.

"I do have to go soon. Can't be late on my first day." He peeled himself from her and looked her in the eyes.

"I'm sorry that happened. Just the stress of moving and starting the new job and everything, I bet."

He kissed her cheek.

"I love you," he said and kissed the other cheek.

"Love you too," Sam whispered back.

CHAPTER 4

J ASON LACED UP HIS SHOES, STOOD UP, AND LOOKED at himself in the hallway mirror. It was his first day of work, and he was supposed to dress business-casual. "Whatever that means," he thought. He slid his thin winter jacket over his white, freshly pressed dress shirt, careful not to mess up his neatly combed hair. He took a final look up and down his monotone outfit.

"Go get 'em, tiger," he said to his reflection with a wink and a finger gun before reaching for the door.

* * *

The elevator opened into the lobby with a ding. As Jason exited, he could see that it was raining heavily outside. He had meant to pick up an umbrella at the market the day before, since he knew Seattle's reputation for being soggy, but he had forgotten. He slowly walked toward the main doors and stopped, staring up at the grey sky, lost in thought.

"There is an umbrella-lending kiosk right over there," the concierge said politely, gesturing towards the little space-age cube just to the side of his desk.

"So that's what that is," Jason responded as he turned to step towards it. As he passed the office, he could see Chester inside, immersed in his paperwork.

"It's free. You just make a profile and enter your credit card information. Then you use your profile to borrow an umbrella anytime you need one. You have 24 hours to return it," the well-dressed concierge instructed.

"Or I'll get charged, I guess," Jason mused.

"That is correct, sir. Twenty-five dollars."

The concierge then turned to accept a package from a courier.

Jason inspected the kiosk, quickly created a profile, and grabbed his loaner umbrella. He thanked the concierge and headed for the door.

As Jason passed the office again, he glanced in to see Chester was gone; the desk clean and tidy.

Outside, Jason opened the black umbrella and headed towards his new office. It was only a 10-minute walk, which was a nice change from his long commute back home. The other significant difference was the weather. Back home was freezing, and there had been snow on the ground for months.

Here, in Seattle, it would snow for perhaps a week or two over the entire year.

But the rain was relentless. And the air was damp and heavy. It wasn't freezing like back in Pennsylvania; it was a trickier kind of cold. It would sneak in under your skin and firmly attach itself to your bones. There it would stay until you could drive it from your body with hot soup or a warm bath.

While the large umbrella protected much of Jason's upper body from the fat drops of rain, it did nothing for his feet. By the time he entered the office building, the rain had soaked his shoes and socks, and his pant legs dripped at the cuffs.

"Damn it," he cursed as he stomped and shook his feet to shake off the offending water. People milled around him, heading to their destinations, seemingly unaffected by the weather.

Leaving a small puddle on the lobby floor, Jason made his way towards the elevator.

There were already several people waiting for the elevator, so Jason pulled out his phone from his pocket. It was a quarter to nine. Jason preferred being early to being on time, or God forbid, late. If he felt like he was running late, Jason tended to become very anxious and irritable. This behavior would inevitably lead to arguments with Samantha, especially since she happened to be a little more laid back than he was.

On several occasions, she had questioned why he would get so upset when getting ready to go somewhere and he felt they were running late. To Jason it was about integrity. Being somewhere when you said you'd be, and doing something you said you would.

"It's kinda rare these days," he would finish.

"Ok," Sam would say, "but we're just going to the mall."

The lobby bell rang, and the elevator opened. It quickly filled like a packed sardine tin, Jason being the last one to fit. He turned around and saw that someone had already pressed his floor's button, lighting it up. The door closed in front of him.

As the elevator rose, each person's individual scent began to mingle into one confused fog. There was a loud talker at the back recounting her "amazing" weekend to her friend. Someone stank of cigarettes, and another had coffee breath. Jason held his own breath as best he could to avoid the offensive aroma. People excused themselves past Jason until they reached the 12th floor. The door opened with a loud ding, and Jason exited gratefully. He inhaled deeply, turned to his right, and moved towards the receptionist's desk.

Clicking away on her keyboard, the young woman said, "Good morning, you have reached Intellican; how may I help you?"

"Oh, hi, I'm Jason. I'm starting to—"

"Just one moment, please, I'll put you through," she interjected, and then looked up to lock eyes with Jason. "Sorry, I was speaking to the caller."

"Oh, of course," Jason fumbled. "Hard to tell, I guess. Sorry about that," he said with a smile.

Her expression softened as her green eyes remained trained on his. She smiled and pushed her hair back over her shoulder. He noticed a Bluetooth headset beneath her long, blonde hair.

"Hiding your headset under all that hair," he teased. She looked down at her computer screen and began typing again.

"So how can I help you, Mr…" the receptionist asked, her tone remaining professional.

"Steele," he offered. "I'm starting today?"

His statement was more of a question, as if to ask if she was expecting him.

"Of course," she replied. "HR will be right out. Please have a seat."

"Thanks…"

"Veronica," she replied.

"Thanks, Veronica," Jason finished. "Good to meet you."

Since Jason was often early, he was used to waiting. He was aware of the fine line between being respectfully early and being intrusive. If you're there too early, it is off-putting to people. Not only that, but it's also a waste of time. Ten minutes is about the max Jason would stretch it. He had it down to a science.

Instead of sitting, Jason slowly meandered around the crystal clean lobby, checking out each piece of art that hung on the wall. The room and art were very modern. The white marble floors shone with fresh wax. The seating, comprised of luxurious, dark-brown leather, was cut at sharp angles and adorned with chrome rivets and feet. The dark mahogany coffee table sat on a fancy white rug with nothing on it but a short stack of tech magazines.

"Jason."

He turned at the sound of his name to see the out-stretched hand of the attractive Human Resources manager.

"Good morning Celeste, a pleasure to see you again." Jason reached out and clasped her hand.

"I hope I'm not too early," he added.

"Not at all," Celeste replied, "You're right on time." She wore her curly, auburn hair in the same way as she had in their video call a few weeks back. As Human Resources manager, she had needed to connect with Jason on a few key points before he moved out.

Although Jason knew Celeste was attractive from the video, she was even more striking in person. She was slightly taller than him in her black heels. Her slender legs ascended up and under her grey pencil skirt. Neatly tucked into the skirt was a crisp white shirt that hugged her torso, exposing every line. A red silk scarf dangled from her fragile neck to complete the ensemble. The scarf matched her lips that spoke, "How are you and Samantha settling in?"

"Getting there!" he responded and followed Celeste's lead as she turned to enter the office.

"It's different, but we're excited to explore the city."

The office was large and open, with groups of neat and tidy sitting and standing desks filling the space past the lobby's frosted glass doors. Some people were there already, working away on their computers. The engineers worked in power groups, each assigned to a specific task. Once a job was completed and optimized, the work went to the senior engineer. The senior engineer was accountable for the quality of the work and meeting deadlines. Individual offices lined the perimeter of the room, assigned to executives and the sales team.

Celeste and Jason walked past the first two groups of desks and came to rest at his space. A welcome basket sat atop the desk, filled with snacks and company-branded swag.

"Wow, look at all this stuff," Jason said as he removed his jacket and folded it around the back of his chair.

"A mug, a polo shirt… sweet hat!" He smiled and looked at Celeste. She smiled back.

"We are glad you have joined us and are looking forward to having you stay." She handed him a manilla envelope.

"Here is some paperwork I'll need you to read over and sign when you have a moment: standard employment contract, banking info, and a non-disclosure agreement. There is also a welcome package with your computer login information. Once you log in, you will move through orientation and training. Right now, though, I'll have you follow me. We need to get your clearance set up at security. It's picture time." She smiled and gestured for Jason to follow. "After that, I will take you over to William's office. He is eager to see you."

* * *

Celeste knocked lightly on the door frame of William's office.

"Good morning William. Jason is here to see you."

"Jason, my man!" William exclaimed with visceral excitement. "Welcome, welcome. How is everything? Settling in well, I hope?"

As William stood up, his black leather chair creaked slightly and rolled backward. He clasped Jason's outstretched hand and gestured towards a chair in front of his desk.

"Please, sit. Do you need anything? Coffee, tea, some water?"

"Oh, no, I'm good, thanks," Jason replied as he sank into the soft armchair. William adjusted his glasses and nodded.

"Fair enough. I'm sure you know where the refreshments are by now if you change your mind later."

William turned to Celeste. "Does Jason have everything he needs so far?"

"For now, yes."

"Thank you, Celeste."

She smiled and nodded, then looked at Jason and smiled again as she turned to leave.

"Thank you, Celeste," Jason echoed as she shut the door.

William's office wasn't any larger than the others, as far as Jason could tell. It held a modern desk with two leather armchairs facing it. Behind the desk was a fancy leather office chair with chrome rivets and feet in the same design as the furniture in the waiting area.

The art was similar too; modern and fierce. As William turned to head back to his chair, Jason noticed long, vertical wrinkles on the back of William's otherwise neatly pressed light-blue dress shirt. Those wrinkles were from sitting and working. Jason wondered how long William had been here already. A hardworking CEO was admirable. Jason didn't want to work for a lazy, entitled millennial.

As a hardworking self-starter, William's reputation had undoubtedly been part of the attraction that led Jason to accept the job offer. William had earned a bit of a name for himself in the tech world, and when Celeste approached Jason to come out and meet him, he was quickly intrigued.

A few years prior, William had stormed onto the scene with the code that remained at Intellican's software base. He had interest from everyone from banks to schools. Private companies and various world governments, including the U.S., wanted to purchase the unique code. William's code had many great applications when you needed to keep information safe.

William sat down and rolled his legs under the desk. He reached for his Intellican mug and took a sip.

"Ahhh, that's good stuff," he said as he put it down. His dark eyes, magnified by his lenses, shifted their focus from his mug to Jason. He leaned back, observing Jason for a moment.

Jason held his gaze, unfazed by the scrutiny.

"Glad you're here, Jason. We've got a lot of work to do to hit our first-quarter targets. I brought you on because I know you can handle the pressure. We have high expectations here. We surround ourselves with the best because we expect the best. That's why you're here. That's why I saved you from that soul-crushing, dead-end wasteland."

Jason smiled and laughed.

"Well, I appreciate the opportunity."

"Appreciate it all you want, Jason, but I'm more interested in how you seize it."

William's cold black eyes pierced through Jason, but he held his boss's gaze.

"Understood," Jason replied as seriously and enthusiastically as he could muster.

"Good. I'm here if you need anything; open door policy and all that. I think you're going to do great here, Jason. Now, get out there and prove me right." Jason nodded as he stood up.

Feeling a little intimidated and very motivated, he went back to his desk.

CHAPTER 5

"NOW BREATHE OUT AS WE MOVE TO WARRIOR pose," instructed the television. "Keep those arms level to your shoulders and chin level."

Samantha stood, glowing in the late afternoon light, breathing out as she found her pose.

"And breathe out as we move into downward-facing dog."

Samantha complied.

Her black lulus and sports bra were damp from the workout. Breathing slowly and deeply, she held her pose. A few drips of sweat landed on the purple mat below her brow. She stared at the small pool and continued breathing.

"Now down to child's pose to finish off our session," the tv commanded.

Samantha knelt slowly, folded herself, and reached out in front of her bowed head. Her forehead rested on the floor as her back glistened. She tried to keep an empty mind, but she couldn't help thinking about her parents. Pangs of longing and guilt stabbed at her guts. They had assured her they supported her decision completely before she left. They said they wanted her to be happy and explore the world.

She struggled with it, though, especially now that her brother was gone too.

"Namaste," the voice concluded.

"Namaste," Sam replied.

She stood up, grabbed the spray bottle of disinfectant, and cleaned her mat. She rolled it up and stored it neatly in the bedroom closet. Samantha caught a glimpse of herself in the full-length mirror and stopped. She twisted and turned, scanning her body and pinching skin here and there.

She peeled her sweaty sports bra over her head, freeing her chest. Her tights were next to go. She stood up again, twisting and turning, inspecting her naked body in the morning light. She reached her arms up, and slender fingers pushed back her dark hair and fastened it into a ponytail. She yawned, stretched, and headed for the shower.

Warm water splashed over her thighs as Samantha entered the shower. It made the rest of her skin bumpy as it instantly tightened into gooseflesh. Her skin eventually relaxed as she engulfed herself under the chrome showerhead. Orange peel and a hint of honey escaped from the frothy body wash and entered her nose. She breathed deeply as the scent invigorated her senses. Her mind painted scenes of a vibrant orange orchard with beautiful Monet skies. There was Jason, waving and smiling. He looked so serene, so happy in his denim overalls and straw hat. So cliché, she smiled.

Samantha moved the pink loofah over her skin as she daydreamed about the orange farm and her lover and their child…

"Hey!" a voice ssaid.

Samantha jumped, and a quick, shrill scream escaped her lips. Suddenly she was aware of reality and her heart pumping like a freight train.

"Damnit, Jay!" she complained. "Scared the shit out of me!"

She panted as she rinsed the suds from her skin.

"Sorry, babe, I called a couple of times when I got in. I didn't mean to scare you. I guess you were daydreaming?"

Jason grabbed a fresh towel from the rack.

"I guess so," Sam responded as she turned off the tap. She stepped into the outstretched towel and Jason's open arms. He grasped her close and paused there for a moment. He released his grip, leaned back, placed a kiss on the end of her nose, and began to rub her arms up and down as if she were a child that had just exited the pool.

"Was it a good one?"

"We were in Florida," Sam mused.

Her eyes were unfocused and distant as she stared at the wall. "In an orange grove. You had a dumb straw hat on."

He smiled.

"And a child."

Jason perked up at the sound of this.

"A child?" he asked.

"A boy," she confirmed. "A little boy with little overalls and a little straw hat just like his daddy." The words flowing from her smiling lips were like music to his ears.

"Oh, shit." Jason's smile was as wide as the room. "Are you saying what I think you're saying?" "Yeah," she mocked, "After just moving to Seattle, I think we should move to Florida, buy an orange grove, and have five babies!"

Jason rolled his eyes, dropped his hands from the towel, and left the bathroom so Samantha could finish up.

"I mean, doesn't sound like a bad plan to me!" he called back as he went to the bedroom to change out of his work clothes.

* * *

"Well?" Sam asked. She leaned over and kissed Jason's cheek on her way past him to the kitchen. "How was your first day?"

She began pulling food from the fridge and cupboards. Jason sat at the island, scrolling the newsfeed on his laptop.

"It was good, yeah. Just got settled in and met everyone. William is a bit intense."

"Oh?"

"Yeah, I guess it comes with being a genius or whatever. He just like, stares into your soul, you know? But that's all good, nice enough guy. Got soaked on my way over there this morning, gonna need some rubber boots!"

Jason took a sip of red wine and continued reading.

"Man, this virus is spreading fast."

"I heard."

"Trump says he's not worried about it, but the CDC is warning that this thing could get out of hand. They say this coronavirus is more deadly than the regular flu. That even healthy young people are dying." "That's a little terrifying," Sam remarked as she danced around the kitchen, mixing and frying and blanching.

"All of the cases are here on the west coast. At least our families back home are safe," Jason said as the screen touched his worried face with an eerie blue glow.

"Dinner's almost ready. Want to eat here or in front of the tv?" Samantha asked. "Jay? JAY!"

Jason jumped sharply as Samantha successfully pulled him from his trance. He blinked away from the hypnotic black writing set against the white screen, looked at his lover, and apologized.

"Sorry, babe. Got sucked in there. Let's eat here. No

distractions." Jason closed his computer while Samantha smiled and loaded their plates up with food.

"Smells awesome," Jason said as the plate's offerings wafted up to his nose.

Samantha topped up his wine glass, filled her own, and sat down.

"It's nice to just sit with you; no distractions."

He cut his chicken and placed a bite in his eager mouth.

"How was your day?"

"It was good, I unpacked more and cleaned. Checked out some job postings and did some yoga. Tried to shower in peace…" she finished.

"Hey, I wasn't trying to scare you!" Jason objected. "It's not my fault you're such a…"

"Such a what?" she retorted.

"Such a…do you hear that?"

Sam looked around with a puzzled expression.

"Uhhh, hear what?"

"It's that damn hum again. Can't even enjoy a goddamn dinner in peace."

His anger intensified as he jumped up out of his stool and marched to the wall separating the living room and bedroom. He put his left ear to the wall.

"Jesus Christ. That's so loud. Like, that's not fucking normal."

Jason took a step back and stared at the wall as if looking at something broken. Something he could turn off or fix to make it stop.

"It's not so bad," Samantha said, "I can barely hear it."

"It's like, the whole place is vibrating. There's no way that's ok!"

Jason's knuckles turned white as his hands became fists. His jaw clenched, and his teeth scraped against each other.

BANG! and another, *BANG!*

"Jay!" Sam cried out. "What the hell are you doing!?" He struck the wall once more as if to subdue the noise.

BANG!

"Jason!" she jumped up and hurried towards him. "Jason?" she said again as she reached out to spin him towards her. He was panting, and a few drops of sweat were streaming from his brow. His wild eyes met hers and his expression softened. His pupils dilated and constricted as he focused on her. His jaw relaxed, and his mouth opened slightly.

"Sorry, babe. I dunno, was just trying to shake something loose in there or something."

"Why did you get so mad, though?" Sam asked.

"I wasn't that mad," he responded, "it's just, this hum, I hate it. How are you just ok with it? Doesn't it drive you nuts?"

"I mostly don't even hear it," she said. "You just have to ignore it, Jay. Don't let it get to you so bad." "I know," he said defeatedly and leaned in to kiss her. "Thank you for dinner. I'll get the dishes."

* * *

"How's Dad?" Sam asked into the phone.

"He's good," her mother replied. "He's a bit worried about you, though. We both are. People are talking about this virus like it's the next plague, and you are all the way out there where it is. You are being safe?" The concern dripped from her words.

"It's not that scary, really, Mom. It's basically just another kind of flu, they say. We are young and healthy. We'll be fine."

Sam tried to reassure her mother, but a pang of doubt marked her tone. "We're keeping an eye on it; hopefully, it will just blow over."

Sam placed her wine glass on the coaster and relaxed back into the leather couch.

"Tell Denise I said hi," Jason said as he passed her in his workout gear. He grabbed his running shoes, laced them up, and headed out the door.

"I'm headed up to the gym, be back in a bit."

The door clicked as it closed behind him.

"Jay says hi," Sam repeated into the phone.

"Hi, Jason," Denise replied. "How is he doing with everything?"

"He's good, yeah. Just settling in. I guess work went well today; he met his team. He just went up to the gym here in the building for a workout."

"Well, that's good he's blowing off some steam. Keeping himself busy," her mother said. "He can get a little…anxious if he has nothing to do."

"Yeah, well, we have a lot going on. Never a dull moment in the city!" Sam said, still a little on edge from Jason's earlier outburst.

"I love you guys," Sam said.

"We love you too. And miss you like crazy already," Denise replied.

"I understand wanting to explore the world and have new, exciting experiences, but I can't help that I miss my baby. Ever since Toby…"

"I know, Mom," Sam interjected. "Thank you for being so

supportive. I miss you guys too. It just felt right, you know? To get away for a bit. With everything that happened. It's like this opportunity came at the perfect time. We're enjoying it here so far. And we can come home anytime if we want to. Nothing is holding us back."

"That's true," Denise agreed. "Ok, well, it's past our bed-time here, gotta get to bed soon."

"I don't know if I'll ever get used to the time difference," Samantha said. "It's so weird, like I'm always running late or something."

"You? Late? Never," Denise joked.

"Ok, talk soon. Love you."

"Love you."

Samantha hit end on her cell and put it down beside the glass of wine. She grabbed her glass, took a sip, and cried.

CHAPTER 6

JASON AWOKE TO THE SOUND OF HEAVY DROPS OF RAIN hitting the bedroom windows. Raining again, he thought. Great.

He reached over to grab his phone, and quick panic shot up his spine. His hand grasped nothing; he looked over to an empty nightstand. Empty except for the lamp. The deep fear of being late for his second day of work worked him over like a fever. His heart began to pump; sweat began to bead on his forehead. Just then, his alarm broke the silence. Relief and confusion swept over him like a wave. "What the…" he muttered.

Jason reached down and pulled on the brass handle of the wooden nightstand. Inside were the contents of what should have been on top of the stand. His phone was there, and the book he had been reading before he turned the light out to sleep was too. Even the short glass of water, a quarter full, peered up at him from its odd hiding place.

"That's fuckin' weird," he said to himself.

Samantha stirred as she made her way back to consciousness. She rolled over and began tracing imaginary curved lines on Jason's naked back. "Morning," she said sweetly.

"Did you put all my stuff in the drawer last night after I fell asleep?" Jason asked.

"What? Why would I do that?"

Sam propped herself up and looked over Jason's toned back.

"Your stuff is in the drawer?"

"I woke up, and the table was empty. Then I thought I slept in 'cause I didn't hear my alarm. Then the stupid alarm went off inside the table. I opened it up, and fuck me, everything that was on top is inside. How?"

"Maybe you put it all in there and forgot," Sam suggested. "No friggin' way. Why would I do that? My glass? Why would I put a glass of water in my nightstand? Doesn't make any sense," Jason complained.

"Well, you must have done it in your sleep then. Either that or we have ghosts," Samantha said.

Jason had already pulled his phone out to silence the offensive alarm. He threw his legs over the side of the bed, took out the other items, and placed them on top of the table. The wood quietly squeaked as he closed the drawer.

"I must have moved it in my sleep. How creepy is that?"

Jason gave the table one last look and headed for the shower.

* * *

"Parasomnia," said a voice from the kitchen.

"What?" replied Jason.

He toweled off the remaining moisture from his naked body, wrapped the towel around his waist, and left the bathroom. In the kitchen, Sam had her laptop open behind the island while turkey-bacon and eggs bubbled and popped behind her on the stove.

"Couldn't hear you," Jason repeated.

"Parasomnia," Sam began again, "is a group of unusual behaviors that can involve talking, walking, or even moving things around while in or transitioning into various stages of sleep."

Jason walked over to see the laptop. He scrolled the document briefly and closed the computer.

"So, I'm just moving shit around in my sleep now. What's next? Sleep sex?" he asked.

Samantha turned the oven dials off and removed the pans of food from the hot burners. She turned and grabbed Jason by the towel.

"Would that be so bad?"

She pulled him closer as her almond-shaped eyes looked into his seductively. He looked down at her plump lips; soft and supple. He smiled, and his dimples popped on his freshly shaven cheeks. Samantha's hand came up to caress his cheek, and she kissed him gently. Her hand slowly traced its way down his neck and onto his bare chest. Samantha's hand continued down and tucked itself into Jason's growing towel.

"I mean, yeah," he breathed. "I'd rather be awake." Sam kissed him once more.

"You better get dressed and eat; you don't want to be late."

She gave his toweled bum a playful smack and turned to finish with breakfast.

"Damnit," he said as he looked at the stove clock. "Wish I could just stay home."

* * *

The heavy rain had subsided into a fine mist so that when Jason arrived at his office tower, he was not completely soaked from the calves down. He crammed himself into the elevator once more, feeling much like a sardine would, he thought, if it wasn't dead and had no feelings. There wasn't much talk from the other elevator occupants this morning, just a heavy kind of silence.

The elevator ding indicated to Jason that it was his stop, and he thankfully exited the claustrophobic box.

"Good morning Veronica," he said as he walked into the main lobby of the office and past the reception desk. Veronica looked up at Jason.

"Good morning, Intellican. How may I direct your call."

Veronica had her blonde hair up into a tight ponytail; a small blue light blinked monotonously from her Bluetooth earpiece. She smiled at Jason.

"Just one moment, please," she instructed the caller and patched them through.

"So you liked us enough to come back a second day?" she asked.

Jason stopped, extended his security card from the retractable lanyard on his hip, and pressed it against the little black box beside the security door. It beeped and the mechanism inside the door relaxed with a click. He grasped the handle.

"So far, so good," he said.

Jason smiled and nodded as he entered for the second day.

The main office area was mostly empty of people. Jason watched as the few people that were there dropped their jackets and bags off at their desks and headed towards the common room.

Jason followed their lead. He removed his coat and hung

it over his chair. He placed his leather courier bag on the floor and headed to the lounge to find everyone still and staring at the flatscreen mounted on the far wall. Concerned faces watched the well-dressed news anchor with BREAKING NEWS scrolling along the bottom of the screen in huge red letters.

"The Centre for Disease Control announced this morning that the Novel Coronavirus, COVID-19, has been labeled a pandemic. Cases are surging across the world, with Europe and the Americas hit hardest. In the U.S., cases are being reported in all states now as thousands of infections have been identified. The global death toll is also rising at an alarming rate. Mass graves are needed to bury the overwhelming numbers of deceased here in Brazil."

The television then showed footage of people in hazmat suits standing around with shovels while large machines cleaned out giant holes in the ground. The frame switched to those same holes, now filled with linen-wrapped bodies; too many to count.

"Jesus," Jason whispered.

The news anchor continued, "President Trump is holding a news conference today at 11 a.m. eastern. We will break to that live coverage as it happens."

The screen continued its cycle of footage showing mass graves and people in hazmat suits. It showed blurred faces of patients in Intensive Care Units, tubes coming out of everywhere as hospital staff acted in frantic movements to save lives. Graphs and numbers that continued to tick upwards flashed across the screen. Global case count, U.S. case count. Global death toll, U.S. death toll.

"I heard Canada is locked down already. Everyone told

to stay inside except for essential needs," Jason overheard the short, stubby engineer in front of him say to the woman on his left.

"How can they do that?" she said. "Don't people have to work?"

"Ok, everyone," a voice said from the door.

It was William. Even though his dark suit was impeccable, he looked like he had not slept. The bags under his eyes were sagging, and exhaustion seemed to have stifled his usual exuberant energy.

"Obviously, by now, you have seen what is happening out there. This virus is spreading faster than people thought it was going to, and it appears more deadly as well. This morning the CDC announced COVID-19 to be a global pandemic. The numbers here in Washington state are surging. And while most people who get the virus will recover without issue, there seems to be a high percentage of people who have difficulty beating it. Hospitals are concerned they aren't going to have enough beds or ventilators for the sick. Our governor will speak sometime this afternoon, when I expect they will introduce a lockdown. China has locked down, and their numbers have stabilized and are in decline."

"Yeah, if you can believe the Chinese," someone behind Jason said under their breath but loud enough for some to hear.

William continued, "Parts of Europe like Italy and Spain have also gone into a lockdown. Only essential services are open: grocery stores, pharmacies, and clinics. Those governments have asked their citizens to stay home except for groceries or if they need medical attention.

"In light of this and in anticipation of the inevitable

lockdown here in Seattle, you are all going to be working remotely, starting tomorrow." William finished his announcement, and a silence deafened the room momentarily. William looked around at his employees. They looked stunned. Then, as if on cue, the voices of almost everyone in the room broke the silence all at once. Everyone was asking questions, concerned and confused. Some were directed at William, some at the person standing to their right or left. Some people asked questions into the ether, rhetorical in nature.

As the voices swelled to a crescendo, fear turned Jason's guts into knots. He sat down among his standing peers to catch his breath. All he could think about was how he had moved Sam thousands of miles away from home only to be locked down and isolated.

* * *

Samantha read Jason's text as the news anchor reported in the background. She had been sitting curled up in her spotless white robe all morning, fixated on the television. Her laptop was sitting open on the coffee table, but she was too distracted to continue browsing the job search website.

She nervously tapped the rim of her coffee mug with her thin gold ring while taking in Jason's words. Being hypnotized by an entire morning of apocalyptic images had Sam anxious and scared, so she was comforted by Jason's text. At least he would be there with her. He would just be in the other room, working, but still here.

She sipped her coffee.

"Just until this thing blows over," he had said in his text.

Maybe a month or two according to the speculation in his

office. Samantha placed her mug back down on the wooden table and turned the tv off with the remote. She gathered her robe around herself, stood up, and went to the window. It was overcast, but the full-length window still allowed for a beautiful view of the harbor.

People were hurrying along on the streets below, milling into and out of various buildings. Samantha stared at them, wondering how many of those people were infected. Just going about their day as if nothing was wrong; breathing, sneezing, and blowing their noses.

She was dreading it, but she knew what she had to do. She turned and headed towards her closet, removing her robe along the way. She hung her robe on the back of the closet door and began to dress. As she was dressing, Sam tried to remember where she had packed her mask. Her father had insisted she bring one. It was common in his culture to wear a mask if you felt unwell, out of respect for others. Samantha loved her Japanese culture; she thought it courteous and respectful, steeped in honor and tradition. As she searched in a duffle bag, her thoughts went to her parents.

Longing squeezed at her heart as memories flooded her thoughts. She rooted through her drawers, looking for the black cloth mask but eventually found it in a small bag towards the back of the closet.

Tucking the mask in her pocket, Sam went to the front door, put on her blue winter jacket, slipped on her waterproof boots, and grabbed her purse. She covered her mouth and nose with the mask and secured the strings behind her ears. Her long black hair fell back down and framed her face. A quick look at herself in the full-length hallway mirror to make sure everything was in its proper place, and she was out the door.

* * *

"Hello, Chester," Samantha said.

Chester looked up from behind the concierge desk. It appeared to Sam that Chester was busy instructing the young concierge in some aspect of his job.

"Oh, Samantha. I barely recognized you in that thing. How are you?"

"I'm well, thank you. Off to the store to get a few things. Pretty crazy, this whole thing."

Samantha gestured to the lobby tv where CNN was playing on mute.

Chester looked up at the tv and back at Samantha.

"Ah yes," he said, "be careful out there. If you and Jason need anything, you'll let me know, won't you?"

"Thank you, Chester. We will."

The mask blocked her smile as she turned and exited the lobby onto the street. People were hurrying up and down the grey sidewalk. Some were also wearing masks. Samantha joined the crowd and headed toward the pharmacy.

"Ow!" Sam shouted suddenly. Pain stabbed her as the impact of the offending pedestrian spun her almost a hundred and eighty degrees. Her shoulder throbbed where the stranger had clipped her.

"What the hell!" she called.

The person didn't acknowledge Sam or the fact that they had almost body-checked her into oblivion.

"Asshole," Sam cursed.

She rubbed her shoulder and carried on through the crowd.

The pharmacy was a madhouse. There were people everywhere, grabbing as much as they could carry. They filled baskets with hand sanitizer, masks, and anti-bacterial wipes. Others had cleared the isles of canned food and batteries, and one lady had a cart with six toilet paper packages.

What was this lady going to do with seventy-two rolls of toilet paper? Samantha wondered.

She grabbed a basket and pushed her way through the people. There were two small bottles of hand sanitizer left, so she threw those in her basket. She saw only one container of wipes. That went into the basket as well. She also grabbed a bottle of rubbing alcohol and a small first-aid kit.

Sam walked over to the next aisle and got some multivitamins, echinacea, and a bottle of vitamin C. She peeked around the corner and saw that the toilet paper was dwindling fast. She hurried over, picked up one package of twelve rolls, and stuffed it under her arm.

"Because I'm not a hoarding bitch," she mumbled to herself.

She walked to the front of the store and began emptying her basket onto the checkout counter. The register beeped as the items rang though.

"Hey!" a voice said behind Sam.

"Hey, lemme buy one of those hand sanitizers off ya, huh?"

The voice belonged to a skinny, middle-aged man who was wearing what looked like a gas mask. His eyes were wild and desperate. He held out a five-dollar bill pinched between two surgical glove covered fingers. The sight of this extra cautious man was both comical and depressing.

"Oh," Samantha said, "Well, you can just have one. No worries."

She pulled one of the bottles of hand sanitizer off the checkout and handed it to the man. He reached out and plucked it gingerly from Sam's palm. He retracted his arm slowly, never taking his eyes from what he coveted.

"Oh, thank you. Thank you," the man said.

He stared at the bottle almost lovingly. Samantha turned from him to find her other items had been through the checkout and placed in a plastic bag.

"Oh, actually, I brought my own bag," Samantha said.

"We aren't accepting those anymore due to the pandemic," the check-out clerk replied.

Sam shrugged and looked down at the screen that was waiting for her action. Tap or insert your card, it instructed. Sam tapped her card and thanked the cashier. With a quick glance back, Sam noted the man had gone. She ran her fingers through the bag's handles, picked it up, and left the store.

* * *

"People are fucked," Jason said. "I mean, five things of toilet paper. How about saving some for someone else? Selfish bitch. And the guy with the gas mask and gloves? What the hell. You'd think we were in a war zone or something."

Jason took a bite of his dinner.

"It was crazy out there," Sam replied. "The grocery store was just as bad. People were loading up on as much as they could carry. I got a little wrapped up in the frenzy myself."

Samantha smiled.

"You know, we have dried pasta and zoodles for the next three months."

"Thank you for doing that, babe. I guess the stores would've been empty by the time I finished work."

"So, how do you feel about working from home?" Samantha gestured at the room behind her that was already set up as an office. Now the room was complete with a work laptop and various "Intellican" paraphernalia.

"It's a little weird 'cause I just started, but it's all good," Jason said. "At least I'll have dry feet all day now."

"At least." Samantha rolled her eyes.

"What!?" Jason feigned his surprise. "Of course, it'll be nice being around you all day too. All day, every day..." he joked.

Samantha's eyes widened, and her bottom lip pushed out in a pout.

"Ah, come on, babe." He put his arms around Sam and hugged her tight.

"You'll be sick of me before too long."

She sank into his embrace and stayed there with her ear pressed against his chest.

"We're gonna be ok right?" she asked. She nuzzled into him further, and his grip tightened.

"Yeah, we are," Jason replied. "We've got each other."

Samantha pulled back and planted a kiss on his lips. "You taste like garlic," she whispered.

"You taste like sex." Jason smiled and showed his dimples. Samantha bit her lip and smiled back.

Jason's muscles flexed beneath his button-down as he grabbed Sam by the waist and pulled her up with him. She wrapped her toned legs around his hips and kissed him again, their tongues wrestling playfully. His hands cradled her firm buttocks as he carried Samantha to the bedroom. He set her down beside the bed, and she began to unbutton his shirt. He loosened his belt and undid his pants. Sam removed his shirt gracefully, and it landed in a pile on the floor.

She grabbed her black Led Zeppelin t-shirt by the hem and flipped it up over her head. With one hand around her back, Jason expertly unfastened the clips of her bra while he continued to kiss her. The lacey, red garment fell to the floor as the pale moonlight from a rare clear evening touched Sam's breasts. Jason grabbed them and squeezed.

"I fuckin' love your tits," he breathed.

The snaps on her pants opened with a pop and they slid to the floor, exposing her tight butt to the world. Jason's pants also fell as Samantha reached down his front.

"Well," she whispered, "What do we have here?"

* * *

The shower hissed, and steam escaped from the bathroom as Jason lay on the bed. His heart, still affected, beat heavily in his chest. He breathed slowly and deeply to relax as he stared out the bedroom window. He watched as thin clouds began slowly shrouding the moon.

His thoughts dwelled on his father and home. He wondered if it had been a mistake coming out here, so far from home. So isolated. If this thing goes wrong, he thought, being in the city would be dangerous.

Jason was pulled from his trance by the ding of his phone; its screen lit the room. He rolled, dropped his legs to the floor, and sat naked on the side of the bed. He grabbed his phone, the blue glow lighting up his features. There was a text from his dad asking Jason how he was.

He replied that all was well, but his new job was now remote and that people were acting crazy in the stores.

Jason sent the text and tapped on the news app.

The virus was continuing to spread. Hundreds of thousands of people around the world were dead. There was a link to a coronavirus counter, so Jason tapped it. The link opened a new browser window that showed a world map with each country color coded based on case count. Below the map was a list of countries with numbers of infected and dead that updated live.

"God," Jason said.

He scrolled a few moments longer, noting the hardest-hit countries. He closed the app and clicked the button on the side to turn the screen off. Jason set his phone down on the bedside table and spread his arms out to stretch.

The steady hiss and sound of flowing water ended as Samantha turned off the shower. Another sound took its place—the sound behind the walls. That monotone hum, droning on. It was there the whole time, of course, just drowned out by the water. He shook his head slightly and stood up. Jason walked towards the wall by the door and pressed his ear against it. The mechanical vibration made him grit his teeth, and he silently cursed whatever was making that infernal racket.

"What are you doing?" Samantha asked.

She had entered the room with one white towel wrapped around her body and one white towel around her hair.

Jason didn't remove his ear from the wall to respond.

"Bah, I dunno. Damned vibration in the wall. It's so loud, not even just the sound but the vibration. Just rubs me the wrong way."

"I only really notice it when you bring it up," Samantha said. "Try to ignore it."

She brushed her fingers across his back as she passed behind him. She grabbed her phone off the bedside table, unplugged it, and lay herself down on the bed. Jason stepped back from the wall and looked it up and down.

"Yeah, I'll try."

He stared at the smooth surface of the wall another moment then turned.

"I'm gonna grab a shower then we should watch a movie?"

"Sounds good."

CHAPTER 7

"**T**HIS WAS A GOOD IDEA," SAMANTHA SAID. She watched the trees fly by her window in a blur. "Yeah, it was," Jason agreed. "So glad to be out of the apartment for something other than a short walk or to get groceries. Was getting a little cabin fever all cooped up in there."

Music was playing quietly over the speakers as they made their way out into the wilderness.

"Mount Rainier looks beautiful from the pictures."

"It's a nice change from staring at the apartment wall for the past two months," Jason said. "And maybe a little fresh air will help me sleep better."

Off the highway, to the left, he could see a large barn. Its massive front doors were open, and inside were cows in pens, feeding on hay.

Beside the barn was a beautiful farmhouse painted white with bright red shutters. Acres of soggy fields sprawled behind it.

"You're keeping an eye on the map, right?" Jason glanced over at Sam.

"Yes, I'm keeping an eye on the map."

Samantha rolled her eyes and grabbed her phone from her lap. She tapped the map app.

"Oh, whoops. We were supposed to take that right back there."

"Are you kidding!?" Jason snapped. "Goddamn it, Sam! How hard is it to keep an eye on the stupid map?" His words bit into Samantha.

"Holy shit Jay, I was kidding! It's like a straight drive until we get there. What's your problem?"

Samantha crossed her arms in a huff.

Blood rushed to Jason's cheeks. Realizing what had happened, he blushed with shame and regret.

"Sorry, babe," he apologized meekly. "I've just been so stressed lately, I guess. I haven't been sleeping well, the new job, being stuck at home all the time, this goddamn pandemic!"

"It hasn't exactly been a cakewalk for me either, you know," Samantha said. Things had started out ok. Jason had his own office space, and she did her own thing. But then, at some point, it stopped feeling like a vacation and started feeling like a prison.

"You used to come out of your office every now and then and say hi and kiss me," she grumbled. "Now your door is shut most of the day, and I have no idea what you're doing in there!"

"I'm working," Jason said.

His teeth grated against each other as he replied. "Are you? It seems pretty quiet in there most of the time. I put my ear against the door the other day and heard only silence. At the start of this thing, all I heard all day was the clicking of your damn keyboard. Now I wonder if you're even alive in there!" Samantha's voice became more shrill as the conversation progressed.

"Don't be ridiculous," Jason said.

His fingers dug into the steering wheel that was now acting as a stress ball.

"And Jesus, you're moody!"

Samantha's almond eyes began to well up until they reached capacity. Tears began to fall down her cheeks.

"It's like I'm walking on eggshells around my own place because I don't know what kind of mood you'll be in at any given time. You come out of your office looking like a zombie, and you haven't touched me in weeks!"

Jason's jaw clenched, and his knuckles turned white from the pressure of squeezing the wheel. He took a deep breath and held it a moment. The SUV rolled down the road to the soundtrack of quiet music and gentle sobs.

After a few minutes, Sam's tears ceased, and her breathing became more even and regular. Her expression turned blank as the scenery rushed by her window—vast swaths of coniferous forest, cut by long, meandering driveways that disappeared into its depths. Small patches of houses and fields sat lonely at the foot of lush, green hills.

Jason's scowl had now softened. His hands relaxed on the wheel as his eyes transitioned from angry little beads to tired, baggy lumps. He looked over at Samantha.

"I'm sorry, Sam. I just haven't been myself lately. I dunno what to say." Remorse colored his words. "I'll be better. I promise."

Jason reached his arm out and placed his hand on Sam's lap. She pulled her gaze from the window and looked at Jason with a deep, fortifying breath. She offered him a half smile.

She placed her delicate hand on his and squeezed lightly. The signs from an increasing number of motels and inns beckoned the couple to come and stay, offering free breakfast and scenic views. But the view they were after was just ahead, past the park entrance.

Jason slowed down and stopped behind a sleek, red sports car next in line to pay the fee. Mount Rainier was not typically busy in early spring, and with the pandemic, it was even quieter.

When it was their turn, Jason pulled up to the visitor center window. The once open window was now blocked by plexiglass with one small hole for talking and one semi-circle for payment. The masked park attendant provided a list of what roads and trails were open and which ones were closed. She also told them that many shops and inns were closed or operating on a massively reduced capacity due to COVID-19. Jason said that they were only planning on spending the day hiking anyway and had packed a lunch, so that didn't bother them much.

The couple pulled away and continued onward towards their destination. The road twisted through the pines at a steady incline. After a few minutes, the trees suddenly broke, and they saw that they had ascended part-way up the mountain range. The road carved out of the side of the mountain was smooth and paved. The odd black line sharply contrasted with the grey rock as it wove its way up and out of sight.

Sam was in awe of the magnitude of it all. They were so tiny compared to the massive rocky formation. The barren peaks and the wild valleys were quiet reminders that life was dangerous. This was easy to forget as people lounged in their climate-controlled homes, rooms full of manufactured furniture, bellies full of imported delicacies.

Out here, though, it was resoundingly clear to Samantha that one wrong step could cost you your life.

"It's beautiful, huh?" Jason said.

"Terrifyingly so," Sam responded.

She cracked the window down, and it whistled. She pointed her nose to the breeze and inhaled a lungful of fresh, mountain air. She exhaled and smiled, allowing the emotions from the earlier conversation to melt away. Samantha sat in bliss, eyes closed, swaying with the road.

Her meditation was interrupted by a shift in speed. Jason slowed down, pulled the vehicle into the parking lot, and stopped. Sam opened her eyes, and with a renewed sense of vigor, collected her things and opened the door.

"We picked a perfect day," Jason said.

He stretched, opened the back, and grabbed his pack. He threw it over his shoulders as Sam rounded the corner. They paused and looked at each other. Jason extended his arms, and Samantha fell into his embrace. They squeezed each other tight and just stood there in the sunlight.

"Ok," Sam said, "let's go see what all the fuss is about."

From their vehicle, Samantha and Jason could see the lake, but it wasn't until they dropped down off the parking lot and onto the trail that the true beauty of the lake struck them.

"Wow," Samantha said.

She paused for a moment to take it in, halting Jason behind her.

"Gorgeous."

She lingered a moment longer, then continued further towards the lake.

Even though there had been a few other vehicles in the lot, there was only one other couple down by the water—a middle-aged woman and her dog. The golden retriever was hard at work, discovering this scent and that, making sure to sniff every stone, log, and clump of grass. Its tail joyfully waved back and forth in the air, stopping only when the animal concentrated on a particularly interesting smell.

Jason and Samantha followed the trail along the lake's bank, past the lady and her dog. The lady waved and the couple waved back. The yellow dog poked its head up for a moment to observe the new visitors, decided they were boring, and continued on its scent-finding journey.

Samantha and Jason stopped and turned towards the body of water. Jason removed the straps of his pack and took in the inspiring view. He set the bag down in the short grass and plunked himself down beside it on an old hemlock log, its trunk worn smooth by the rear ends of a thousand travelers. Sam pulled off her pack and sat down beside him.

A few feet ahead of them, the ground fell off into the shallow, sky-blue lake.

"I guess that's why they call it Reflection Lake," Samantha said.

The lake's quiet surface acted as the perfect mirror for the monstrous peak of Mount Rainier, which resided just beyond the evergreen forest on the opposite side. A perfect doppelganger.

"A fitting name for sure. Not very inventive, though."

Jason smiled at Samantha, hoping that things were ok again. She smiled back. She usually smiled easily, and even though Jason didn't feel like the smile was fake, it certainly was a little forced.

"My brother would have liked it here," Sam said.

"Toby?"

"No, my other brother."

The sarcasm was thick as she rolled her eyes.

"I just meant," Jason began, "he wasn't really the out-doors type. That's all."

Jason slowly traced lines into the dirt with his shoes. "Just because he didn't want to join you and your hick buddies to go kill defenseless animals doesn't mean he didn't like the outdoors," Samantha said.

Toby was a touchy subject, so Jason kept quiet and continued to trace his lines.

"I just miss him, that's all."

Samantha inhaled a deep breath and enjoyed the sun on her skin. A smile spread across her face as she remembered her brother.

"He was a good guy," Jason said. "It's a shame."

He took in a breath and stood up.

"Shall we explore some trails?"

Jason turned to Sam, extended his hand, and bowed slightly in the knightliest way he knew how. She took his hand and used his weight to pull herself up from her wooden seat. The sudden strain almost set him off balance, but he quickly recovered.

"Let's do it."

They slipped their packs onto their backs and headed out into the wilderness.

Branches broke the sunlight into a thousand pieces as it fell to the forest floor. Shadows danced on the gravel path as Jason and Samantha navigated along the well-manicured trail. Pine needles quietly rustled as the cool breeze gently caressed them with endless ebbs and flows.

Small streams fed from waterfalls created by spring thaw

gurgled and splashed in the distance. Jason listened as the forest's smooth ambiance was constantly interrupted by a soft tweet from a bird or sporadic chatter from a cautious squirrel.

The forest teemed with life—a stark contrast to the city's concrete, metal, and plastic. And not a moment's peace from the noise. The traffic, the gadgets, the…hum. And even with all those people there…they didn't seem alive.

Jason wasn't thinking of the thousands in Seattle who had died in the past two months from the coronavirus. He was thinking about all the people who seemed dead on the inside. You know, the ones with the blank look in their eyes and muted energy. Those people who are just killing time, going through the motions until death claimed their bodies to join their minds.

Jason shivered.

"He *was* a good guy," Samantha said.

Jason figured her thoughts were still dwelling on her brother; deep in thought, she hadn't said a word since they left the lake twenty minutes prior. Jason learned a while ago that it was best to let her have that time and wait for her to talk when she was ready.

"But so unhappy," she continued. "So fundamentally unhappy. On the outside, it looked like he had everything: a family who loved him, a decent job, a cute boyfriend. He had food and shelter and love! He basically had everything! Sad, selfish bastard." Samantha spoke in heated tones, but she didn't cry. She had no more tears left for him. Samantha wasn't even angry at Toby anymore. She just felt empty about it, like a question that would never be answered, a space too large to fill. Sam would never know why her brother took his own life; she could only speculate. "Maybe he never really got over being bullied. You know, about being gay," Jason said.

He knew to pick his words carefully. Even though he would never want to hurt Samantha's feelings intentionally, sometimes, he just did.

If he worded a thought in a certain way or said something dumb without thinking it through first, he would pay for it. He just wanted to help; to be there for her. After Toby hung himself, Jason quickly realized that it was usually best to say very little about it.

"Maybe," Samantha said.

She had thought about all the whys a thousand times.

"But we were always supportive, our family. We suspected it anyway, years before he came out. When he did come out to us, we kind of just shrugged and said ok. The people who mattered loved him. Accepted him."

Samantha and Jason's pace through the woods slowed as they talked.

"Those fuckers at school, though," Jason said. "Just wouldn't let it be."

Samantha sighed and stopped. She allowed her bag to drop from her shoulder, knelt, and opened the zipper. She pulled out a sweaty water bottle and took a long drink, then handed it to Jason with a quiet little burp.

"Excuse me," she said. "It had been years since all that stuff in high school. Toby seemed over it. In a good place. Who knows though, I guess."

Jason handed the bottle back to Sam. She capped it, threw it back in her bag, and zipped it back up.

Suddenly, a quick, loud shriek broke the stillness. The couple looked around for the source.

"What the hell was…"

Then another slightly longer scream pierced the woods.

"This way!" Jason leaped forward and began to run towards the sound that had sent chills up his neck.

"Jay, wait!" Samantha called.

She hesitated a moment, looked around, then followed.

Not far up the trail, Jason found a small path winding towards where he thought the scream had come from. He unclipped the leather sheath of his hunting knife attached to his belt and pulled it out. He did not open the blade but held it ready.

He galloped through the woods with animal-like precision. Many years of chasing prey through his family's hunting grounds guided his actions.

Ahead he saw what looked to be a person crumpled on the ground. Maybe they fell and broke their ankle, Jason thought in a flash.

The person was still, though, unmoving, as far as Jason could tell.

As he approached the fallen hiker, he called out, "Hey! Hey, are you ok?"

No response came from the pile of clothes on the forest floor. Then Jason saw why. His gallop slowed to a jog; then, he stopped dead in his tracks.

Blood.

So much blood covered the front of the jacket, it was difficult to see that it should be light blue.

"Ah, Jesus."

Jason's face contorted into an expression of horror and confusion.

"What the fuck."

Jason had witnessed many animals dead and dying, some by his hand. Often, when he had shot a whitetail deer back in Pennsylvania, it would take off running through the bush. Jason would track it by broken saplings and blood splatters until he came upon the animal, dead or dying.

Jason was no stranger to the terrified eyes of a dying animal; he had watched the life drain from them many times, leaving dull, matte black globes.

This hiker's eyes were no different; eyes that once held life were now dull and unseeing. He heard Samantha's footsteps on the ground behind him and quickly turned to try to stop her from seeing the mess.

Jason leaped towards Samantha, grabbed her tight, and spun her around. His eyes once again fell on the hiker's lifeless face. Her bloodshot eyes stared dully up at him.

Jason shivered.

Samantha broke free of Jason's weakened grasp and spun to face the source of his concern. There, in the dirt and leaves, was the second dead body Samantha had ever seen.

"God," she whispered. "What happened?"

Instantly, Jason's parasympathetic system took control of his actions. Jason instinctually opened his hunting knife and scanned the surrounding trees for the vicious predator that could have done this. Blood rushed to his core; his limbs twitched in anticipation. He reached a hand back to keep tabs on Sam as he pivoted, pointing his now opened knife forward in his other hand, locked in a defensive pose. As he slowly turned and shuffled in a circle with his back to Sam and the hiker, he thought maybe he would see a wolf or bear staring at them coldly from a distance. Jason cocked his head back and looked up at the canopy. Perhaps he would spot a cougar hiding up high in the branches, ready to pounce when the moment was right. Jason wondered if cougars even lived in this park.

Satisfied that he and Sam were in no immediate danger, Jason knelt beside the body, reached for the blue jacket, and pulled it open. He couldn't help but register the warm, sticky sensation on his fingertips as he did.

"I dunno," Jason said. "I don't think an animal did this, Sam."

Samantha already had her phone out, checking for service. One bar. She dialed 911, tapped send, and hit the speaker function.

"Damnit!" she said anxiously. She paced around nervously, phone extended to the sky, wishing for the call to go through.

Success.

"911, what's your emergency?" asked the voice on the other end.

"Uhh, umm, we're in Mount Rainier National Park and, hiking, and there's someone here, dead, we heard a scream…"

Samantha fumbled with her words as they came in quick, abrupt spurts.

"Where exactly are you?" the voice asked.

"Uhm, Reflection Lake. Well. Between Reflection Lake and Paradise; on the trail. I don't know. It's hard to say."

"Ok, stay on the phone with me here; I'm sending police now."

Samantha did her best to calm down by taking a few

slow, deep breaths. Jason continued to scan the forest, on guard against any danger.

"Ok."

Samantha stood with her legs pressed tightly together, arms half crossed with her phone in one hand. Her stomach turned as she stared down at the dead woman; the tranquil beauty of the forest sanctuary now defiled by the scene in front of them.

CHAPTER 8

I T TOOK SOME TIME FOR THE POLICE TO FIND THE couple in the forest. Jason and Sam had made their way off the main trail where they found the hiker and had become disoriented from the events.

The officers finally did reach them and quickly led the couple back to the main trail and out to the police cruisers for questioning.

Before long, more police arrived in marked trucks and vans. The trucks hauled four-wheelers that police quickly unloaded and drove into the woods. The police unloaded tents and equipment from the vans, setting up a command station in the gravel parking lot. More officers and deputies entered the forest, weighed down with packs and gear.

A deputy offered Samantha and Jason each a paper cup filled with hot coffee, which the couple eagerly accepted. Then they were separated by the police to be questioned in-dividually—to corroborate their stories. The couple each sipped their drinks as they answered questions and pro-vided their statements.

The events were fresh in their minds; the images vivid and alive. When Jason had finished his statement, he was left standing by the cruiser, staring into the woods. As time went on, he started to worry about Sam and began second-guessing himself. Had he left crucial bits of the story out?

He hadn't.

Samantha's statement took longer than Jason's because her tongue felt fat and lethargic in her throat, causing the words to leave her lips awkwardly. She hesitated in her speech as if she feared that uttering the words would make all this more real. When she had finished, the officer opened the door for her and she got out.

She walked towards Jason with the foil emergency blanket wrapped around herself, more for comfort than warmth.

"How are you?" Jason asked as he moved towards her.

"Good. Ok," Sam said. "The cop said she would give us a ride to our car."

The short ride to their SUV was silent except for the brief, sporadic chatter over the police radio. The car pulled into the lot beside Jason's SUV and parked. The officer unclipped her seatbelt and threw open her door. She opened the back door so Sam and Jason could exit.

"Here is my card. We will be in touch. We recommend not leaving the state."

The cop gave the couple a stern look and closed the back door of the cruiser behind them.

"Also," she said, "you may want to speak with a shrink or someone. Might help." She nodded, got back in her car, and headed back to the investigation. Jason and Sam stood quietly, half bewildered. Their SUV was the only vehicle left in the darkening lot. The last piece of sun sat waiting on the horizon, finally becoming engulfed by the dusk.

* * *

There was little conversation on the two-and-a-half-hour drive back to Seattle. The radio played music quietly while the engine droned along at its constant pitch. Samantha longed for a hot shower and warm food.

She tried, without much luck, to block the disturbing images from her thoughts. It kept playing over in her mind: she is running along the dirt path. A thin branch clips her cheek with a poker of hot pain, the evergreens blurring in the background. She sees Jason; he looks shaken. She sees the body, lying there, motionless. The jacket an odd shade of reddish blue. Over and over the memory played, like a short, disgusting video clip stuck on a loop. She shook her head to clear her mind and hoped that the thoughts would fall out of her ears.

She looked over at Jason.

He was gripping the wheel with both hands; not anxiously, just alert. His eyes were relaxed in the darkness, occasionally pierced with daggers of light from oncoming vehicles. He hated driving at night.

They weren't even supposed to be out this late, Sam thought. Jason didn't have to wear glasses when he drove, but that's usually the only time he wore them. Just a small prescription. Just enough to sharpen everything up. Samantha liked how he looked in his glasses and secretly wished he'd wear them more. So smart and sophisticated.

He seemed calm now as the passing headlights rolled over his face. His beard was getting long—she liked that too.

No need to shave in lockdown, he had said. Samantha had had to put her foot down just before their trip. The scraggly beard needed a trim. He knew it too, so Jason hadn't put up a fight.

Samantha remembered how she had complained that he trimmed too much. Such complaints seemed so trivial now.

Who cares how he looks? she thought, as long as he loves me.

Jason could feel Sam's gaze. He looked over at her. "You ok, babe?" he asked.

Samantha nodded, placed her hand on his leg, and gave it a gentle squeeze.

"Love you."

* * *

When Sam and Jason entered the apartment, the familiar smell of home hit their nostrils. Sam felt safe for the first time since the incident as she closed and locked the door behind her. They threw their bags down in the entranceway, removed their jackets and boots, and left it all in a pile on the floor.

They peeled their clothes off as quickly as they could, leaving a trail of garments on their way to the bathroom. Samantha cranked on the shower, and water burst from its head. She tested the stream and waited.

Jason opened the lid of the toilet and sat down with his phone in his hand.

Deciding that the temperature was acceptable, Samantha entered the shower.

Jason stared at his phone.

"Like, how do we tell our parents about this? How do we tell anyone?" he mused.

He set his phone down on the counter, uninterested in the device.

"I don't know," Sam replied. "That was insane." Samantha

stood still under the shower, allowing the hot liquid to soak her hair. The warm water saturated her thick, dark hair and poured over her naked body. She worked to block the video loop from her mind and relax, visualizing the memories running from her body and down the drain.

* * *

"Are you serious?" Denise asked.

The bad phone connection broke her voice up a little at the end.

"It was so crazy, Mom," Sam said. "Like, I'm still shaking a bit."

Samantha had called her mother shortly after dinner. The thought of reliving the day's events had almost stopped her, but she needed to hear her mother's voice. Samantha didn't usually complain to her parents. Nor did she tell them about the more challenging parts of her relationship with Jason. She didn't want to affect how her family felt about him and didn't want them to worry.

So what if she and Jason had a few fights every now and then? Doesn't everybody?

But this phone call was different. Samantha needed to dump verbal diarrhea into the cell.

Sam told her mother about the beautiful drive and the stunning lake; how the trails had smelled like Christmas. She described the fresh mountain air and how it had a way of energizing you. Then, how it was all ruined by what they found in the woods.

She didn't go into any great detail about it.

She didn't describe the pooling blood or the sick feeling

she had gotten when she saw the hiker's colorless, agony-stricken face and dull eyes. Samantha did say that the hiker was a middle-aged woman and that she could have been beautiful when she was alive.

Denise had put her phone on speaker at some point during the conversation, and Sam's father's voice came through now and then, his tone colored with shock and concern.

Sam's phone was also on speaker, allowing Jason to chime in when necessary. He did his best to sound strong; he wanted Denise and Ken to feel confident that he could take care of their daughter.

After reassuring her parents several times that she and Jason were fine and just needed a good sleep, Samantha ended the call. She set the phone down on the coffee table and stared up at the tv's flat, black screen.

Jason had stood up and gone to the window. He looked out into the night, gloomy and quiet. Since the lockdown started two months prior, the streets had been nearly empty.

What used to be a bustling harbor front was now reduced to a scene of boarded-up windows and empty sidewalks. Closed down businesses meant less people. The shortage of people meant fewer trucks. Fewer trucks meant that the area was much quieter than it had been before. The quiet streets would have suited Jason just fine, except the stillness outside only magnified the presence of the hum inside.

He stood staring out the window but entirely focused on the dull, constant drone of the sound behind the walls. The sound vibrated its way under his skin and cut into his bones like a dull saw. Jason's jaw mashed his teeth together as his hands balled into fists. He hated that hum. He hated this apartment for housing that hum. He hated that he felt so helpless against it. It wasn't some broken piece of code he could fix or a carburetor that could be cleaned. It was something beyond his control.

"Come to bed." The words broke his trance.

Samantha's gentle touch upon his elbow calmed his taut muscles and beckoned him to the bedroom.

* * *

Samantha was so drained from the day's events that she was unconscious soon after her head hit the pillow. Jason lay beside her, staring at the ceiling, wishing he could follow suit.

He jealously listened to her nose whistle every time she breathed in.

Behind that was the hum.

It was the only ambient sound in the apartment; all other sounds lived and died, but not the hum. It was constant and unrelenting like a freight train. It was the blank, grey canvas waiting for the painter's brush to add color and shape.

Shapes and images.

Jason tried to keep the pictures from his mind as he lay there, taunted by the hum. The memories passed through his thoughts, brilliant flashes of green and crimson. He saw the hiker's pale, tortured face. Her dull eyes stared into his soul, searching for darkness, and finding it.

CHAPTER 9

"**G**ODDAMN IT, CHESTER," JASON SAID. "IS THERE really nothing you can do about that damn noise?"

"We had the electrician come in and inspect the electrical room, and everything was normal. I asked him about the hum you mentioned, and he said you can hear a lot in the walls in these older buildings. Not much for insulation, since it doesn't get very cold here. In other words, not much I can do, I'm afraid." Chester's blue surgical mask bounced up and down as he spoke. Seattle had instituted a by-law requiring people to wear masks in public, enclosed spaces. Jason didn't like it much, but he agreed with the principle—to protect others from your germs.

Chester sat behind his sturdy desk. Near the front was a big bottle of hand sanitizer with a pump nozzle on top, the opening caked in dried chemicals.

Hand sanitizer was everywhere now. Jason had even seen a homeless guy outside a local grocery store, bent over with his mouth around the spout, chugging away gleefully.

"It's so bad," Jason said meekly. "It's affecting my sleep and my work." He paused. "Hasn't anyone else in this building complained about it?"

Chester shifted in his seat.

"Well, no," Chester replied, then brightened. "Have you thought of headphones?"

"So I'm just supposed to wear headphones all the damn time?"

"I'm sorry, Jason. Just trying to help."

"It's not your fault, Chester."

The big man eased back into his chair a little, relaxed by Jason's decision to take a more calm tone.

"It just sucks."

Jason was pacing in front of Chester's desk as he spoke. "Yesterday was a rough one, and I just wanted a good night's sleep, and it didn't happen, headphones or not."

Chester sat watching his visitor pace. Jason stopped walking when he realized complaining further would solve nothing, said his thank-yous, and excused himself.

"Well, what did Chester say?"

Samantha was busy in the kitchen, cooking something for lunch. The tip of her ponytail gingerly touched the collar of her white robe as she worked.

"He said there isn't a damn thing he can do about it."

Jason removed a small bottle of sanitizer from his pocket and squeezed some into his hand, a wholly unconscious habit now. He kicked off a shoe, but before he could remove the other one, a knock sounded loudly at the door. Jason turned in place and opened it.

A tall, uniformed police officer stood in the entrance, a blue surgical mask blocking his mouth.

"Good morning," he said. "Are you Jason?"

"I am."

"Do you mind if I come in for a moment?"

"Not at all."

Jason opened the door further and stood to the side to allow the officer through. The officer took a few steps into the apartment and removed his hat. "Ma'am." He nodded towards Samantha.

She turned the dials on the stove off and removed the cooked food from the hot burners.

"Hello," she replied. "How can we help you, officer?"

"Detective," the man said from under his mask. "Detective John Topp."

Detective Topp scanned the room as he spoke.

"It involves the incident yesterday at Mount Rainier."

"Did you find out what happened?" Jason asked.

Detective Topp looked at Samantha.

"Well, when you called 911, the boys in Ashford quickly set up a checkpoint on the road in front of their station. That's the one you folks passed through."

Sam and Jason both nodded, hanging on the detective's words.

"Well, another one was set up where the one-twenty-three comes out at highway twelve on the other side of the mountain. These are the only roads in and out of the park."

Jason wished Detective Whatever would get to the point.

"Turns out one of the fellows that passed through the checkpoint was the husband of the deceased. We have a warrant out for his arrest."

"A warrant?" Jason asked. "You mean you haven't arrested him yet? Why not!?" Detective Topp gave him a look that indicated he didn't like it when people raised their voices at him. Jason quickly calmed himself.

"Sorry, I just don't understand."

"Well, you see, it's hard to arrest a man you can't find. It took a little time to identify the woman, and once we did, I went over to her house to speak with the husband. He wasn't there obviously, and once I saw his name on the list of stopped motorists at the checkpoint, I called in for a warrant."

"He knew you'd be looking for him," Jason said.

"He likely rushed home knowing he had a bit of a head start, grabbed whatever he could, and took off," Detective Topp said with a nod. "Have you seen this man?"

The detective reached inside his jacket pocket and pulled out a picture. Jason and Sam leaned in to get a better look. The face on the photo didn't look much like a murderer: a plain-looking guy with light, curly hair and a well-trimmed beard. Jason admonished himself for admiring a murderer's facial hair. "No," Jason said.

Samantha shook her head.

"Didn't see him running away? You said in your statement to police that you found the body only a minute or two after the scream."

"To be honest, I didn't know what to think when I got there," Jason said, trying to piece it together in his mind. "I couldn't believe it. I'd never seen anything like that, and the first thing I thought was that a bear or mountain lion did it. I looked around real good, but I didn't see anything. The bastard must have run off quickly."

Detective Topp seemed satisfied with the answer.

"Well," he said, "We consider this man to be armed and dangerous, and even if you didn't see him, he might have seen you. Best to stay inside and keep an eye out when you do leave the apartment. Keep this picture, and here's my card. Call me if you see him or anything suspicious."

Detective Topp handed Jason the items and put on his hat. Samantha took a step towards the cop. "Should we be worried?" she asked, frowning with concern.

"I would say the chances that he saw you are low. I'd say the chance he would come looking for you is also low. He's probably on his way to Canada, looking for a way to get in. Just a precaution until we get him. Keep an eye out."

With that, the detective tipped his hat and left, the door clicking shut behind him.

Jason looked at Samantha. Not knowing what else to do, Samantha went over to the stove, turned it on, and finished cooking lunch.

"Are you going to call your dad today?" Samantha asked. She set a plate of food down in front of Jason and one at her setting.

"What? And tell him we witnessed a brutal murder, and the guy is still out there and maybe coming for us next?"

"Ok, dramatic," Sam said.

She grabbed a bottle of white from the fridge before settling into her place.

"Wine with lunch?" Jason said.

She popped open the woody cork and filled her glass halfway.

"Considering the situation, why not?" She shrugged.

"True enough; hit me."

Jason's portion finished the bottle, and Sam put it down with a clunk.

"Cheers!" she said as she lifted her glass towards Jason.

"Cheers," he echoed, grabbing his glass and touching it to hers with a ding.

"I'll have to call. Tonight I guess; not looking forward to that."

"Why not?" Samantha asked.

"I'd rather just not talk about it anymore. Every time I

retell the damn story, it's like reliving it again. I'm trying to kill the bloody images from my brain, not picture them even more."

Samantha nodded in agreement and took a sip of wine.

* * *

"There's another one of those protests today," Sam said.

After lunch, she had made her way to the couch and turned on the news. Samantha and Jason weren't nightly news watchers back home; they would perhaps watch occasionally to see what was happening in the world. Recently, it seemed the only thing happening in the world was the pandemic, but the couple still tuned in to see the latest at least once a day.

Jason was busy cleaning up the kitchen and doing the dishes.

"What's that?" he called over the noise of the faucet.

"Another anti-mask protest at City Hall today," Sam repeated. "God forbid you wear a mask to try to stop the spread of this thing."

Jason rinsed the last piece of dinnerware and set it down in the drying rack. He shut off the chrome tap and picked up a dishcloth to dry his hands.

"Lots of people are upset right now. A lot of people are out of work and starting to get desperate. They think the virus is a hoax."

Jason hung the towel over the oven door and walked over to the couch. He sat down beside Samantha and put his hand gently on her back. He started tracing large and small circles with his fingers through the fabric, knowing the simple action would comfort her.

"That's so dumb," she said. "I don't understand what the government would gain by making this up."

"I dunno, babe," Jason said, still scratching Sam's back. "Some people think everything is an elaborate plan to control them or take away their rights and freedoms."

As they spoke, their eyes never left the screen. Samantha had muted the volume earlier, but they didn't need to hear it. The message had been the same for months; people are dying. All the pertinent numbers scrolled continuously along the bottom of the screen anyway.

That is what everyone was watching. How many people infected; how many dead. The numbers climbed by steady jumps at what used to be a shocking rate but had now become mundane.

"The new normal," they called it.

Jason didn't like that term much.

"These idiots don't realize we are already pretty well controlled. Hell, we all have a number assigned to us. The government knows where you live, what you do. Google knows what you look at, and even what gets you off. Anti-vaxxers talking about the government injecting you with whatever. If the government wants something in you, they'll just put it in your damn drinking water! I don't get it. People don't believe that there could be a simple explanation for things: A damn flu virus mutated and is killing a bunch of people, and our dumbass civilization is having a hard time stopping it. Why is that so hard to believe?"

Jason's voice grew raised and hot. His already short temper had been whittled down to a nub over the past few months. Samantha put her hand on his thigh and squeezed softly.

"It's ok, Jay; those dummies can go and breathe on each other all day, get sick, then realize that maybe a mask isn't such a bad thing after all."

Jason took a breath.

"Yeah, you're right. Let Darwin take care of it."

CHAPTER 10

Jason's eyes slowly opened. The bedroom was bright. A good way to start off the week, he thought. His eyelids were heavy and burned his eyes when he blinked.

Did I sleep at all? he wondered, trying to figure how many hours he may have slept. Not enough, was usually the answer lately. The weekend felt unreal and distant as he focused on his job and the tasks that he needed to complete. Jason pulled the comforter off himself and sat up on the edge of the bed. He habitually reached for his phone as he stretched out his body.

Nothing there.

He looked over, and once again, the tabletop was clear, except for the lamp that stood lonely in the corner. He sighed and opened the drawer. Inside it was everything that he had left on the bedside table when he turned out the light last night. Jason stared blankly at the contents of the drawer for a moment, knowing that this was the fourth or fifth time this had happened since they moved in.

The new normal, he thought.

"I'm fucking losing it," he said as he removed his belongings from the drawer and closed it.

"What's that?" Sam said as she entered the room.

She went to her dresser and pulled out some clothes.

Jason looked over at her and said, "Nothing, just talking to myself."

No need to bring it up again, no need to add more worry.

Jason watched Samantha strip off her robe and hang it on the back of the bedroom door. He watched her half-naked body as she walked back over to the dresser where her clothes lay on top. She pulled on her black tights and flipped a loose, grey sweater over her head.

"But you aren't even sleeping," she said sarcastically. "Very funny," Jason shot back, painfully reminded twice now that his sleep problems seemed to be getting worse.

Samantha had been letting Jason know with increasing frequency that he had been talking in his sleep until about a month ago. Then she had stopped, and this was the first time she had mentioned it in a while. Not because he hadn't been doing it.

The new normal, he thought again.

"I'm headed out to the store to grab a few things; do you need anything?" Sam asked.

She walked over to Jason and ran her fingers through his hair as he sat shirtless on the bed. He looked up at her.

"I don't think so, thanks though."

Samantha bent down and planted a kiss on Jason's cheek.

"Ok," she said, "I'll see you in a bit."

* * *

It took twice as long as it used to do anything now, Samantha thought. She set her bags down in the hallway and locked the door behind her. Lines everywhere, as stores only let a few people in at a time. You had to sanitize and put on a mask. Then sanitize some more. Her hands had become dry and cracked from the rubbing alcohol. You had to consider things never considered before, like; should you get another package of TP even though you just got one? Or should I get some canned fruit, you know, in case Armageddon happens, and we'll need vitamin C to stave off the scurvy?

She removed her jacket and shoes and brought the bags to the kitchen, where she set them back down on the floor. She grabbed the container of antiseptic wipes from under the sink and began the ritual of wiping down the groceries; cream for the coffee, the egg carton, and a small bag of oats. There were also some cosmetic items, including a new mascara and lip balm. She spent a small fortune on shampoo since her hair was so long and thick.

Samantha threw the used wipe into the garbage with the plastic grocery bags. She felt guilty about that, but stores wouldn't allow people to bring their own bags from home right now. Such a waste, she thought. She placed the groceries in the cupboards, grabbed her cosmetics and shampoo, and headed for the bathroom. She paused briefly outside the closed door to the office.

Silence.

There was no clicking of the keyboard, no phone call or video chat, just silence.

Lately, Samantha had noticed long stretches of silence behind that door, getting longer and longer with each passing day. One day last week, maybe Wednesday, she thought, Sam didn't hear anything from the room once, all day. She hasn't dared ask Jason about it, though. He had been so stressed lately and on edge. The slightest thing could set him off. The past weekend was supposed to be a break from this. To help him relax and feel better. She had planned an escape from the confines of the small apartment so they could breathe and regain some of their vitality. That plan was bashed to hell when they found that hiker murdered. What was supposed to be a break from their waking nightmare had ended up adding to the horror.

Samantha continued to the bathroom and dropped off her things. She set the makeup in the drawer and the shampoo in the shower, then turned around.

"Oh!" she gasped. "Jesus, you scared me!"

Standing in the doorway was Jason, a blank, tired look on his face.

"Jason?" she asked and reached out to touch his arm. The pressure of her hand on his arm snapped him out of it. His eyes cleared, and confusion furrowed his brow.

"What… what the hell?" he said. "Fucks going on?"

"I don't know!? I just got back from the store and was putting stuff away, and then all of a sudden, here you are! Were you sleepwalking!?"

Samantha sat down on the toilet, her hands trembling slightly.

"Shit. I dunno," Jason said meekly.

He looked at the floor, at his hands, then at Sam.

"I guess I fell asleep at my desk? And fucking sleepwalked in the middle of the day? Who does that!? Jesus!"

Jason stormed off into the office and slammed the door behind him. Samantha sat staring at the wall, disbelieving what had just happened. She sat until her hands steadied and she was confident that she could walk without fainting.

Samantha headed to the kitchen, noting the steady click, click, click of the keyboard from behind the office door as she passed. It was almost lunchtime, and although she wasn't all that hungry, the only thing Samantha could think of to do was cook some food.

Chicken and peppers sizzled and popped in the hot skillet. The smells awakened Sam's appetite as she stood watch over the stove. She hoped the scent would rouse Jason too and coax him from that room. Even if it did, though, it was unlikely that she'd be able to talk to him. Lately, when he did come out for lunch, it was always brief. He would silently grab something and recoil back to his lair like some strange, recluse animal, closing the door behind him. Even at the end of the workday, he would exit the office looking like death warmed over. It would take some time and a few tries to extract a lucid conversation from Jason.

As if on cue, the office door opened, and Jason emerged.

"Sorry I scared you before," he said sheepishly as he stopped and leaned on the kitchen island. "I just spent the last hour researching sleep clinics. Most are closed due to the pandemic, but I found one; Dr. Luu. I made an appointment, but it's not until Friday afternoon."

Jason sat down, planted his elbows, and rested his heavy head in his hands.

"Oh, alright, good. I was going to suggest seeing someone, but…" Sam trailed off.

"But what?"

"Well, you've been super moody and stressed, and even before last weekend, it was hard to talk to you. I didn't want to upset you. Especially now, after what happened at Rainier."

"Yeah, I'm sorry, babe," Jason said.

"It's ok," Sam said as she walked around the island to hug him.

"I just want you to feel better."

Samantha cupped Jason's beard in her hand and bent down to kiss him. She looked into his eyes. "Love you."

"Ditto," he said with a smile. "Smells good. Fajitas?"

Samantha grabbed her tongs and filled four flatbreads with the steaming chicken and sweet pepper mix from the hot pans. She finished each one with shredded cheese, a spoonful of sour cream, and a squeeze of lime. She set the plates down at their places on the island, turned around, and opened the fridge to find the orange juice.

"Thanks," Sam heard as she reached for the carton. She turned around to see Jason already headed back to the office. He disappeared inside and closed the door.

He had still talked more than most lunches, she thought.

Samantha sat down in a disappointed heap and began to eat.

* * *

Samantha hadn't had any luck finding work, and the pandemic only made it more difficult. With not much else to do during the lockdown, she had become somewhat of a Sudoku wizard. She could spend hours on the couch pouring over the black and white grids, analyzing the lines, determining which numbers went where. She usually worked on the puzzles on the couch, from where she could hear whatever sounds were coming from the office. It's not like she was eavesdropping; she had nowhere else to go, and the apartment was small.

She was working through a challenging puzzle when her phone vibrated. Someone was calling—unknown caller. She pressed the talk button. "Hello?" she said into the speaker.

"Hello, Samantha?"

"Yes."

"It's Detective Topp from the Seattle PD. Do you have a moment to speak?"

"Yes. I do."

"Well, ma'am, sorry to bother you, I tried Jason's phone but no response. Anyway, we picked up our man trying to cross the border in Idaho, so you can relax now."

Relax, Sam thought. What's that?

"Oh, that's wonderful news, Detective. So glad to hear it. It's been a very stressful experience, to say the least. Any idea why? Why he did it?"

"Well, I can't really comment on an ongoing investigation, but I can say that in the last two months since lockdown began, we've seen a sharp increase in domestic violence calls. Some of those calls have ended in a similar way to that hiker up there, if you catch what I'm sayin'."

"That's terrible."

"Anyways," Detective Topp continued, "we may need you two for the trial when it gets underway; might have to testify or whatnot. We'll let you know."

"Whatever we can do to help," Sam said.

"Ok then, you all have a good rest of your day now." The call ended, and Sam's phone switched from the call screen back to her wallpaper. It was a picture of her and Jason just before they left from Pennsylvania. They both looked so excited and happy. Ready to take on the world. How things change, she thought.

She rose from the couch, went to the office door, and listened. It was quiet inside. She knocked gently. No answer. She tried again, with the same result. Samantha reached for the brass doorknob and turned it slowly. The door opened to her push. Inside, the clear, white light of the LED bulbs in the ceiling lit up the room in an unnaturally bright way. Loose papers and thick books sat in piles on the desk surrounding the closed laptop and Jason's sleeping torso. He was bent over, with his arms folded, cradling his head as he slumbered. Samantha looked at him with pity. She wished he were sleeping better. She wanted him to be happy and playful like he used to be. Their relationship had never been perfect, but it wasn't whatever the hell this was.

Samantha longed for home. There, she had family and friends; a support network. Jason did too. He would have support from family and friends as he worked through this sleep stuff. They were just so damn alone here. She flicked the light switch off and closed the door.

* * *

"That detective called today," Samantha said as she finished up in the kitchen that evening.

"Oh?" Jason asked. He was sitting on the couch, his glazed eyes staring at the tv screen.

"They caught the hiker's husband. He was trying to get into Canada, I guess."

Jason looked over at Samantha.

"Did he say why?"

"Why the husband did it?"

"Yeah."

"Not specifically, no. He just made a comment about an increase in domestic violence since lockdown began."

Jason looked thoughtful for a moment, then looked back at the tv.

"Hope he hangs."

Jason's words were like venom, filled with hate.

"I don't think they do that here, Jay."

Samantha walked over and took a seat on the couch beside Jason. He wasn't so out of it tonight, she thought. Must have been a good nap.

"Either way, one less thing for us to worry about." Jason put his feet up on the coffee table and leaned back into the soft couch cushions. Samantha shifted and leaned into his side. He put his arm around her and changed the channel. The twenty-four-hour news channel popped on and as if on cue. The banner scrolling at the bottom of the screen was showing statistics of domestic violence in America, comparing incidents before and after the pandemic. Samantha stared at the numbers, wondering what would drive people to the point of hurting those they love.

* * *

Sam's eyes opened. It was dark except for the lights from outside that cast shadows in their room. The haze softened as her eyes grew accustomed to the darkness. Her heart beat steadily in her chest, pumping blood all through her still body. She closed her eyes again and took in a deep breath meant to relax her. Instead of falling back to sleep, though, Samantha's eyes opened again as she realized Jason's body was not weighing down the mattress beside her.

She looked over to where he should have been, and saw only the cover, pulled back, and a headless pillow. This was not the first time Samantha had awoken in the middle of the night to find herself alone. Sometimes the kitchen light would be on, and Jason would be sitting at the island, helping himself to a midnight snack. Sometimes the bathroom light would be on, and she would hear the steady stream of piss. Other times though, no lights were on. Which usually meant that Jason didn't need the light; he was sleepwalking.

Sam sat up and looked around the room, half squinting in the dark. Her eyes scanned the shadows until she finally saw Jason, standing with his ear firmly planted against the wall. He stood motionless. His eyes were open but unseeing. He just stood there, listening to the hum. The first time Samantha had witnessed this odd behavior, she called out to him, asking what the hell he was doing listening to the wall in the middle of the night.

He hadn't answered.

She had hopped out of bed to scold him for being so crazy about the damn wall noise but had stopped dead in her tracks when she saw his face; his eyes. She had known then that he wasn't awake. She had crawled back into bed with an uneasy feeling that hasn't gone away since, but only reduced in severity.

Now though, Samantha thought it sad that she was getting used to this. Jason used to just talk in his sleep a little, mumbling mostly. Then, he started sitting up and having full conversations. Now he would get out of bed and do the weirdest shit.

Samantha lay back down on her side so she could keep an eye on the eerie sight. She couldn't go back to sleep now, not until he came back to bed. So she lay there for what seemed like hours until Jason finally straightened up, turned, and walked back to bed. He got in and pulled the covers up and over himself. Samantha lay staring at his back. She realized how odd it was that if she didn't wake up to witness these events, she would never know they happened at all.

CHAPTER 11

THE NEXT MORNING JASON AWOKE FEELING MORE rested than usual. The dull achy headache that usually greeted him in the morning was gone, and his mind felt fresh for the first time in a while. Samantha was already up, so he sprang out of bed to go and find her.

Samantha was bent over the bathroom sink wearing a tiny white tank top and red booty shorts. Her bum cheeks jiggled playfully from the back-and-forth of her purple toothbrush. Jason crept up behind her, wrapped his arms around her torso, and pressed his body into hers. She paused for a moment and then stood up straight, breaking his embrace. Jason took a step back. Samantha spat mint foam and ladled water to her mouth with her cupped hand to rinse. She gargled and spat the water into the sink, watching Jason in the mirror as she wiped her mouth with the back of her hand.

"You're in a good mood," Sam said, noting Jason's smile.

"Actually had a good sleep last night, I guess."

"Was that before or after you were sleepwalking?" She hadn't been mentioning it lately, but his sleep problems were affecting her sleep now too. It seemed like every night, Jason unknowingly woke her up. Apparently she wasn't even safe from it during the day either, if Jason happened to pass out in his office while working. Jason's smile faded.

"What'd I do this time?"

"Nothing new. Standing with your ear up to the damn wall."

Concern marked his face, and he raised his hand to his mouth to work on his pinky fingernail, the only one with a small piece left to chew.

"Damnit, babe, I'm sorry. I don't want to do it. I wish I didn't. Can't help it, really." He paused. "Hopefully, this Dr. Luu can help me sort it out. But I don't know what I can do until then, though."

Jason left the bathroom and headed for the bedroom, dressed only in his boxers. He grabbed some sweatpants and a Pink Floyd t-shirt and put them on. Samantha followed.

"I came into the office yesterday, and you had passed out on your desk. Dead to the world."

"So you must have turned the light off then. I woke up in the dark wonderin' where the hell I was. I didn't remember shutting off the light, but then again, I've been doing all kinds of shit that I don't remember doing lately."

Jason walked over to the bed and sat on its side.

"I put all the stuff in my night table when I sleep now—almost every night. Why the hell do I do that?"

He stared at the nightstand as if trying to figure out a complex puzzle.

Samantha joined him on the bed and put her arm around him, stroking his arm gently.

"We'll figure it out, Jay." She smiled. "Maybe you just need more naps on your desk to start feeling better?" Jason let out a short chuckle.

"Afternoon naps, huh? I could be into that."

* * *

Samantha was sitting upright on the couch, trying to figure out how to make her hands move with the knitting needles in order to create, hopefully, a beanie. On the coffee table in front of her sat her opened laptop with a how-to video flickering away. She paused it, tried to mimic what the teacher instructed, not wholly confident of the result, then replayed the same part of the video again to make sure.

It was a slow process, but she was determined to learn how to knit. It kept her brain and hands busy, leaving less time to think about the insanity that they had been experiencing.

"Hold the work and needle in your left hand firmly," the video said, "then loop under and back to complete a stitch."

Samantha did as instructed, entirely focused on the work. In the background, the clackity-clack of Jason's fingers hitting the keyboard was constant from behind the door. Amazing what a little sleep could do, Samantha thought.

"Ok, that's enough for today," Samantha said to herself as she set down the needles and closed her laptop. It was almost 4:30 p.m. Jason would finish work soon and would likely be up for a walk today, she thought.

Samantha pulled out her phone and began to browse her socials. Besides getting groceries, going for walks was their only escape from the apartment. The lockdown in Seattle had been strict. Nothing was open for entertainment: no movie theatres, no concerts or bars. The government shut down everything deemed "non-essential," which included the space needle and all the tourist traps.

Samantha wondered how these businesses would survive. It had been months of lockdown, and even though businesses had been forced to close, it wasn't like their bills suddenly stopped. Companies would still owe rent and taxes, utilities, and upkeep. The cost of doing business didn't stop just because the income did.

Samantha felt sorry for them. She and Jason supported small companies where they could, but there wasn't much they could do aside from ordering takeout now and then. With a single income and no job prospects for Sam, the couple had to be careful too; their bills wouldn't stop either. So many people were facing the same and worse. With businesses shut down, the unemployment rate had skyrocketed, and people were broke and scared.

There had been protests and riots, calling for the government to open things up again, the main sentiment being that the damage of unemployment was worse than the damn virus. Suicide and domestic violence rates had increased exponentially.

Whether due to the protests or not, the news had lately reported that the government was looking at opening some things up soon with advanced safety protocols. Samantha was on the fence about how she felt about that, but she did know that a vaccine needed to happen pronto.

The clicking stopped, and after a moment, Jason appeared from the office. He looked over at Samantha. She was bent over her phone, her neck almost parallel to the floor. Her eyebrows were scrunched up to create a deep V between them on her forehead, indicating she was deep in thought and somewhat perplexed.

"You're gonna hurt your neck all bent over like that." Samantha looked up, startled. So engrossed in her phone, Samantha hadn't heard the clicking stop or seen Jason out of her peripherals. She straightened her neck and back in a stretch and set her phone down on the table.

"How was work?" she asked.

"Productive. Got a lot of shit done."

Jason walked over to Sam and kissed her on the cheek. "Shall we go for a walk?"

* * *

Samantha and Jason left their building and stepped out onto the sidewalk. The air was mild and briny. Dark, dense clouds threatened rain from above, but so far, the day was dry. They headed down towards the harbor, a favorite path of theirs to take. Some days they would see harbor seals poke their shiny, dark heads out of the water to have a look around. If the couple were lucky, they would walk past a fishing boat cleaning their catch and get to see a lighthearted show of seals arguing over which one gets the next scrap of fish guts thrown from the boat.

The harbor was fairly quiet when Jason and Samantha arrived. A few boats swam lazily along the channel. An older couple passed by, holding hands and looking like something out of a Nicholas Sparks movie.

"So cute!" Samantha gushed and grasped Jason's arm tighter.

The two continued their stroll along the seawall. An amazing assortment of boats and yachts were moored to the wooden piers. There were bright, brand-new white cruisers. There were beat-up old sailing boats, not pretty, but seaworthy. Mixed in, here and there, were even a few interesting-looking houseboats. One was two stories, painted red with yellow window frames. Four giant windows allowed people to see right into the small, basic rooms.

"How'd you like to live there?" Jason asked with a light elbow to Samantha's arm.

"I don't know," she said, eyeing the floating house suspiciously. "I think I prefer solid ground."

As they rounded the corner on the paved pathway, three cyclists sped past, dinging their bells in warning. Jason watched them go, lost in thought about how he ought to be getting more exercise and if maybe he should give biking a go.

"Hey, watch out!" a voice shouted.

Suddenly, Jason was ripped from his thoughts by the squeal of brakes and a flash of pain. A cyclist had been moving way too fast from behind the cedar hedge, and when he merged with the pathway, he had collided with Jason with a thud. The cyclist flew over the handlebars like some spandex-clad seagull, clipping Jason's shoulder, and landed on the pavement in a heap. Jason spun and fell back hard against the pavement, hitting his tailbone and skinning his palms. The bike flipped a complete three-sixty, bounced once on its tires, and crashed to the ground with the mechanical sound of its chain rubbing against the sprocket.

The bike came to rest with the back tire spinning wildly, Samantha looking on in horror. By some stroke of luck, she had emerged unscathed. The cyclist groaned, and Jason remained sitting on the ground, bewildered.

"Jason!" Sam half screamed, "are you ok!?"

She moved to squat beside him where he sat, dazed; his arms stretched out behind him, propping him up.

"Yeah, shit. I think so," Jason replied. "Jesus Christ." He looked over at the lump of cyclist and felt anger begin to simmer in his guts.

His shoulder throbbed, and it hurt to move. Jason got up

anyway—slowly. Once up, he took stock of himself, checking bones for breaks and feeling around in his shoulder for the source of its pain. Nothing broken or dislocated, he diagnosed. Jason rolled his shoulder gingerly and took a step toward the cyclist. A shooting pain suddenly poked at Jason's brain, and he staggered. A faint, high-pitched note sounded in his ears. Jason instinctively reached up with both hands and held his head, working to hold his skull together. The ringing grew louder, and he plugged his ears with his fingers to stop the sound, but it was no use. The sound was already inside. Jason shook his head as his vision began to blur. He stopped and stared blankly down at the cyclist. The quickly oscillating waves of the ringing modulated and slowed inside Jason's head. The sharpness became a dull throb. It became familiar as slow waves pulsed behind his eyes. The hum hammered slowly on his eardrums as he stared at the source of his physical pain.

"I said what the fuck were you thinking, dude!?" Jason's voice erupted from pain and anger.

The cyclist was crumpled over, face down, holding his stomach. He groaned. The cyclist wore a black helmet that Jason could see was cracked and barely holding on around the man's head. Good thing he was wearing that helmet, Jason thought, that would have cracked his skull open like an egg.

"Hey, dickhead!"

This time Jason reached out his leg to coax the cyclist to roll over and face the man he had almost killed. The cyclist did roll over onto his back, and a grating half groan, half gurgle escaped his throat. Jason bent over the man with a clenched fist ready to fly.

"You stupid son of a bi—"

Jason stopped cold.

His fist softened and slowly lowered. The noise in his mind cleared and only a headache remained. The cyclist was just lying there, half conscious, staring at the sky without seeing it. A trickle of blood was running down his forehead and began to pool in his right eye socket. His right arm looked like a question mark, broken in at least two places, Jason guessed. The cyclist's right leg looked like it was screwed on backwards.

"Babe, call 911."

Samantha snapped out of her daze, grabbed her phone from her back pocket, and dialed. Samantha and Jason couldn't do much but stand there and wait with the broken cyclist. He was beaten up pretty bad, but he was conscious and not bleeding to death from what they could see. People started to gather around, curiously horrified by the scene. Jason absently switched back and forth from rubbing his shoulder and tailbone while not-so-politely reminding people to stand back.

The cyclist lay clutching his broken arm to his body, his forehead beaded with sweat and mixed with blood. Shock had fully consumed him, and he had the look of a trapped and terrified animal. Jason knew that look and pitied the man.

"You're alright," Jason said, half lying. "The ambulance is on the way. You're alright."

Samantha was sitting on a nearby bench, watching the scene intently. She was concerned for both men and thankful she had somehow been spared. It felt like life was working in slo-mo as she sat there on the bench, waiting for help. Two bike cops rolled up and took charge of the scene. They asked Jason what happened and took his statement.

He couldn't help feeling a little déjà vu.

When the cops were satisfied, they talked to Samantha. She gave her account, and the cops moved on to other witnesses. While the cops were taking statements, the paramedics arrived on the scene. They were wearing thin white hazmat suits, respirators, and plastic face shields.

Extra precautions due to the pandemic, Jason thought.

Two sets of blue gloved hands grabbed the stretcher from the truck, and the two paramedics placed it down beside the hurt cyclist. They checked his vitals, secured his arm, and slid a flat board under his body. Then they strapped him in and lifted him onto the stretcher. From there, it was up the path, into the meat wagon, and off to the nearest hospital. It was a whirlwind of action, like something out of a cartoon. They were gone as quickly as they had come, leaving Jason with his bruises and bloody hands.

CHAPTER 12

"**L**et's get you cleaned up," Samantha said as she closed the apartment door behind them. The paramedics had asked Jason if he was ok and he had said yes, but now the adrenaline had worn off, and he felt like he'd been hit by a freight train. He kicked off his boots and headed for the bathroom. Samantha ran warm water into the sink and grabbed the rubbing alcohol from beneath it. Jason winced as water poured over his scraped palms. He winced even harder and let out a yelp when Samantha dabbed at his palms with an alcohol-soaked cotton ball.

"Son of a bitch!" he hissed.

"You're ok."

Sam grabbed another cotton ball for the other palm, held it to the open bottle, and inverted it, allowing the cool liquid to leak out. The other hand wasn't as bad, and Jason was thankful for that.

Samantha grabbed the bottom of Jason's shirt and pulled it up over his head. She spun him around to inspect his shoulder. It was red and already showing signs of bruising. Little purple lines marked his skin where the weight of the cyclist had pulled it in an unnatural way.

"It's like I'm cursed or something," Jason said.

"Cursed?"

"I dunno. I just feel like nothing has gone right since we got here. This place is just kicking my ass."

Jason sat down on the toilet seat and hung his head, holding his palms up so the air could dry them.

"Speaking of which, how is your bum?" Sam asked.

Jason pressed the back of his hand against his tailbone.

"Not too bad, I guess."

"Have a warm bath, and when you're done, we'll ice you down," Sam said as she turned on the tub faucet. Jason nodded and removed the rest of his clothing, leaving it all in a pile on the floor. Samantha planted a small kiss on his lips and bent over to pick up the clothes.

"There's blood on your shirt from your hands, I guess," Samantha noted as she inspected the clothes. "I'll see if I can get it out."

She watched as Jason carefully entered the half-filled tub, then she headed to the laundry room.

* * *

"The guy almost killed me," Jason said into the phone. He was lying on his back on the leather couch, propped up with some pillows. The news flashed on the silent tv screen. Samantha was turning something into deliciousness in the kitchen. A savory aroma hung in the air. Jason adjusted the icepack under his shoulder.

"Came outta nowhere and kablooey! You shoulda seen him fly, Dad." Jason paused. "He got all fucked up; his arm was just dangling there in like three pieces."

"Jesus," the voice from the speaker said. "You're good, though? Nothing broken?"

That was how Jason's dad measured the severity of a situation. Broken bones? No? Then you're fine, just walk it off.

Ron Steele was a bit old school in his approach to parenting; in his approach to all things, really. He was stern but fair and made sure he did the best he could do. Ron had never coddled Jason; he had wanted his son to grow up strong and independent. Ron supposed he had succeeded; his son was so independent that he had moved two thousand miles away. Ron wondered if his son might have stayed closer to home if he had felt more love from his father. Perhaps Ron could have made more of an effort. He did tell his son that he was proud of him, and often. Ron used to think that was good enough.

Jason adjusted the icepack again; this time, he moved it under his tailbone. He was wearing loose, black track pants and an old beat-up t-shirt. He figured he looked about as good as he felt.

"Yeah, I'm alright, Dad. Just a bit beat up. Sam's taking good care of me."

"Thank God for her," Ron said. "Don't know what you did to land that one, son, but you better not screw it up."

Ron's voice was light and joking, but they both knew the truth of his words.

"You're too kind," Samantha called from the kitchen. "Ah shit, she heard me, huh? Just as well. Hey sweety, how are ya?"

"Good, Ron. A little drained from the day, but it could have been worse."

"That's the truth," Jason added, remembering the cyclist on his back in the middle of the cement path, holding his smashed-up arm close to his body protectively, his hip on sideways, staring into the abyss with that freaked-out look on his face. Jason pictured the crimson pool of blood as it slowly formed in the man's eye socket. Each blink added a touch of deep red to the white of the man's eye until the entire sphere had finally been covered, drowned in its own ocular cavity. Jason snapped out of it and noticed Samantha plating dinner.

"Ok, Dad. Looks like it's dinner time."

"Alright, glad you're ok. Take it easy," Ron said, and Jason touched the screen to end the call.

He sat up just as Samantha lowered their plates onto the coffee table, the delightful smell of green Thai curry wafting up to Jason's nose. He breathed in deeply.

"Mm, mm, mm! That smells good!"

Samantha and Jason sat together, hunched over their food, taking in mouthfuls of Basmati rice soaked in curry sauce. The coconut milk supplied sweetness to the fresh, savory vegetables. Jason poked at the tofu.

Samantha had unmuted the news, but there was no new information. Even the increasing case count and death tolls had become mundane. It was all just part of life now. It was a sad truth, but until the large pharmaceutical companies developed a vaccine, not much could be done other than wearing a mask and sanitizing the skin off your hands. Every night, the main argument that took center stage seemed to be: What was worse? A portion of the population contracting and dying from the virus, or the financial ruin and mental health disintegration of the population, leading to depression, anxiety, and suicide? In other words, was the cure worse than the disease?

These debates showed the news anchor in the studio, with a person framed in a picture-in-picture, broadcasting from their phone or webcam in their home office or kitchen. Jason wondered how many of them even wore pants. He wouldn't, he thought. The debate raged on as one expert on mental health argued that more people would die from suicide and domestic abuse than from COVID-19. Another expert said if people didn't stay in their homes, the death toll could easily double in the next three months. The news even featured guests who believed that their fundamental freedoms and rights had been stripped away by being forced to wear a mask. Samantha thought these people must live privileged lives if their biggest complaint was having to wear a mask in public. The news also reported, very infrequently, about a small fraction of people who believed the whole thing was a government plot, designed to use fear to control the population; to give up their rights for more security. Some thought the pandemic was a lie; others believed the government distorted the data to make the situation appear worse than it was. God knows why.

Samantha raised the remote in her hand, and with the push of a button, the screen went black and silent.

"That's about as much of that I can take today."

She put the remote down and looked at Jason. "How's the shoulder?"

Jason's icepack was half melted and lukewarm. "Not bad. Gonna eat some more Advil before bed. Hopefully, I'll sleep; I feel exhausted."

"Same," Samantha responded.

She grabbed the pack from Jason, got up, and headed to the freezer to throw it in.

The couple had been in Seattle for over three months but were still adjusting to the time change. They spent their whole lives existing in the eastern time zone before moving, and jetlag was still very much a factor in their lives. Three hours makes a huge difference. In their new home, if they went to bed at 10:00 p.m. (an unheard-of thing for Jason), their bodies thought it was 1:00 a.m. When they woke at 7:00 a.m., their bodies thought it was 10:00 a.m. This discrepancy made Jason feel like he was always running late—an extremely stressful thing for a man who hated to be late. Samantha enjoyed the change, however. She liked going to bed early and waking up in the same fashion, and the move had forced Jason to follow suit. Although, she thought, she wished he slept better.

* * *

"Want a fresh icepack?" Samantha asked as she entered the bedroom. Jason was lying on top of the covers, one leg crossed over the other, wearing only his grey boxers. His right shoulder looked swollen and angry in the lamplight. At the other end of his arm, his hand rested on his abdomen. His left hand cradled the back of his head on the white pillowcase as he stared at the ceiling thoughtfully. "Hm? Oh, um, no, that's ok. It'll just get the bed all wet and nasty. I took some painkillers and muscle relaxers, so that should do the trick."

Samantha nodded and crawled into bed beside Jason. She rolled to her left, plugged in her phone, and set it on the nightstand. Then she rolled to her right and kissed Jason on the cheek.

"Minty fresh," he said.

Samantha clasped her hands together under her cheek, nestled into the pillow, and closed her eyes.

Jason wondered how anyone could sleep like that. She looked like a peaceful cherub, angelic and serene. He fought back the jealousy.

"Love you," they said, almost in unison.

Jason squinted, and a quiet grunt escaped his lips as he adjusted himself to get under the comforter. Samantha didn't like to sleep with a sheet; she said it always ended up crumpled and in a ball at the foot of the bed, so why bother? Just the comforter was fine with Jason unless it was really hot; then he wanted nothing but a thin sheet covering his nakedness. But it didn't get that hot in Seattle anyway, so the point was moot.

Jason looked over at his nightstand as he reached for the lamp switch. He paused with his hand holding the long, dangling chain that controlled the light, staring at the items on the tabletop. With a sigh, Jason let the chain go and opened the drawer. As quietly as possible, to not disturb Samantha, he stored everything in the drawer and slid it shut. Might as well, he thought and turned out the light.

The dull ache in his tailbone and throbbing pain in his shoulder kept Jason awake until the painkillers and muscle relaxers found their way into his bloodstream. He relaxed into the mattress as the pain reduced to mild discomfort. His eyelids were heavy, and his eyes burned behind them, dry and tired. In the background, the bedroom walls vibrated their constant note. Jason focused on the hum until he could hear nothing else.

His earphones were in the office, and he was too tired and sore to retrieve them, so he just lay there, half asleep and listening.

"Hummmm… Hummmm…"

Jason hummed along with the noise, matching its pitch. A D-minor, he mused, or maybe a G. Jason chuckled softly to himself.

"If you can't beat 'em, join 'em," he whispered and chuckled some more.

Samantha stirred and rolled onto her other side, facing away from Jason. His eyes opened wide, and he held his breath as he watched her reposition herself, praying he didn't wake her.

All clear, he thought and closed his eyes again. The hum carried on, unwaveringly relentless in the dark room. It mingled with Jason's thoughts. Thoughts of the crumpled cyclist, broken and bleeding from his eye. The crimson pool filled the eye socket and then overtook his face and began to swirl. Around and around, the thick, red blood turned in his face like some fucked up toilet bowl until Jason fell in.

* * *

"Jay?" A melodic voice said. "Jason."

He stirred to the sound of Samantha's voice. His eyes opened, and the room was bright and fresh: a new day. Something was off, though, his fuzzy thoughts determined. Confused and groggy, Jason cocked his head to see Sam standing over him, fully dressed. "What the…" he began.

Jason realized he was on the floor, curled up beside the wall. No pillow, no blanket; completely naked except for his boxers. Jason lay huddled up in the fetal position, trying to figure out how and why he came to be in this precarious position.

"For someone who says they hate that noise, you sure seem to want to listen to it a lot," Sam said as she straightened up.

Jason looked around, half bewildered, then sat up, resting his back against the wall. He could feel the hum's vibration prick his skin as he became suddenly aware of the thumping ache that tortured his right side.

"I do hate that fucking noise," Jason snapped. "It's driving me mental."

"Obviously," Samantha replied.

"I didn't want to wake you, but I have an appointment, so I have to go. I'll pick up a few things from the grocery store too. Do you want anything?"

Jason just shook his head slightly. He looked a mess. His hair had grown out and was shaggy and unkempt—it had been a while since he visited a barber. Were they even open? Damned lockdown. Damned pandemic.

His achy muscles had fallen victim to slight atrophy from complacency and smothered by a layer of fat that had become increasingly thicker since the lockdown began. The gyms had closed at the beginning of the pandemic. The thought of sweaty, muscle-bound sardines all piled on top of each other, panting, grunting, and coughing must have made the decision easy for the government. Jason had tried to continue his fitness regime at home with videos from the internet, but had lost interest quickly.

Stress and lack of sleep made him lethargic and moody, and the last thing he wanted to do was get all sweaty and out of breath. The stress and lack of sleep showed easily on his face. Plump, dark bags hung from under his eyes as he stared at nothing. "Ok, I'll be back later. Maybe a shower will help you feel better? You have time before work."

Samantha turned and left the bedroom, leaving Jason sitting against the wall in a daze, unmoving.

CHAPTER 13

CHESTER SMILED AND WAVED AS SAMANTHA PASSED his office in the lobby. His door was open.

"How are ya holding up, dear?" he said from behind his tidy desk. Samantha stopped in the doorway. She usually cringed when strangers called her by a pet name—it just seemed so fake—but a name like dear, coming from a man like Chester, just felt normal—good even. He had a favorite uncle vibe to him that Samantha had liked right away, and she enjoyed his presence.

"Good," she said, half lying, but who answers that question truthfully? *How are you? Good.* That's how it was supposed to go.

The big man stood and walked closer, but not too close; there was a pandemic and social distancing to consider. He stopped about four feet away; his mask bobbing as he talked.

"And Jason?" He eyed her reaction to the name closely.

"He's good too…a little stressed and a bit stir-crazy, I think," she said with a polite smile that Chester couldn't see under her surgical mask. Cautiously satisfied with her answer, Chester's posture relaxed a bit.

"He seemed a bit stressed when I spoke with him the other day. Hopefully, this thing blows over soon, and we can get back to normal. You know what helps me?"

Chester raised one emphatic bushy, grey eyebrow.

Samantha raised both of hers. "What's that?"

"I do a little bit of meditating in the morning."

He raised his hands as if to fend off a physical attack. "I know, I know. I'm not the Dalai Llama or anything. I haven't attained enlightenment or gotten 'woke', as my niece would say, but it does help a lot."

Samantha knew he was the favorite uncle and suddenly remembered the time.

"I will suggest it to him; we both could probably benefit from it. He laughs when I ask him to do yoga with me. Oh well. I have to run, though, Chester. Thank you for the suggestion and concern; we are fine, really."

Samantha bowed slightly, and Chester returned the gesture in kind. A slight nod or bow had become the new handshake in this touchless world.

Her appointment wasn't far from the apartment; just a few blocks. She took her time, walking casually in the sunlight. Usually, it was so wet and miserable that everyone hurried everywhere to avoid the weather. Today though, there was a calmness to the people in the streets. There was an easiness to the conversations Sam overheard as she passed by. There were more vehicles now than at the beginning of lockdown. The government had started allowing more places to open due to pressure from small businesses and their patrons. You couldn't go to the movies yet, but you could get a haircut.

Jason could use a visit to the barber, she thought. He could use a lot of things; some exercise, some family and friend time, a chill pill. She hoped that this sleep doctor would provide insight into what was going on with Jason and maybe help—even just take some of the pressure off, because if not, she feared something was going to pop.

Samantha's thoughts dwelled on Jason and his troubles until she reached her destination. She entered the lobby and waited for the elevator. When it came, she entered with one other person. Two people were the maximum allowed now, for safety. The elevator took them up quickly. The man, dressed in an old brown suit, stood as far away from Samantha as possible. Any further and he'd be halfway up the wall. The most challenging adjustment Sam had to make was getting used to the way people looked at each other now. With fear. The tall, balding man with a shit-brown suit and black-rimmed glasses was looking at tiny little Sam as if she was going to beat him up and take his lunch money.

But that's the way it was now.

Fear dripped from people, some more than others, but it was there on all people. You could almost smell it.

The elevator slowed and halted on the eighth floor. The door opened with a digital ding. Samantha exited and read the black sign behind glass on the opposite wall. Another digital chime and the elevator door closed behind her. 806—Dr. Greene, with an arrow pointing to the right. Samantha turned and headed in the direction of the office.

Room 806 opened up into a small waiting room. There was one other person there, sitting on a plastic chair in the corner, staring at her phone.

The waiting room had obviously been stripped of its former, typical furnishings. Cloth-lined, padded chairs had been swapped out for non-porous, blue plastic set three feet apart. There were no side tables; no magazines to leaf through while you waited. Gone were the wooden block toys and pop-up books for children or the young at heart. The room looked bleak—painted institutional yellow and empty. The receptionist was seated behind plexiglass to the left.

Sam walked over to the window and instinctually pumped sanitizer into her hand and massaged it in. The sharp smell of alcohol touched her nose.

"I have an appointment with Dr. Greene," Sam said through the small holes in the glass.

"Insurance card?"

The receptionist was a young man with short, brown hair and a small face that his mask covered up to his eyeballs. Samantha slipped the card under the glass and waited for the nurse to poke about on the keyboard. He looked up at Sam while typing, then back down to finish his work. He slid the card back to her and asked her to have a seat.

"We'll call you when the doctor is ready."

"Thank you."

Samantha turned and picked a seat that wasn't close to the other waiting room occupant but wasn't the farthest one away either.

After only a few short minutes, the door to the offices opened, and the nurse got up with charts in hand. "Betty?"

The woman sitting in the corner gathered her phone and purse and headed to the open door. "Room one, please," the nurse said as Betty disappeared into the hall.

"And Samantha."

Samantha stood up, phone in hand, and walked to the door.

"Room two, please."

Samantha walked into the hallway, found her room, and sat down in the small plastic chair beside the bed. She didn't want to get on the bed unless she had to. She looked around the medical room. On the wall hung the machine for taking blood pressure and the thing they stick in your ear. On the counter were jars filled with white cotton balls and wooden tongue depressors. A small laptop sat on a short desk with the password screen open. The bed was clean and sterile; white paper extended across its surface. A sudden knock startled Samantha.

The door opened. Dr. Greene entered wearing her white lab coat, a stethoscope around her neck, holding Samantha's freshly printed chart. "Samantha?"

Sam nodded.

"Ok, let's find out if you're pregnant."

CHAPTER 14

I T WAS LATE MORNING BY THE TIME SAMANTHA ARRIVED home. After the doctor's appointment, she had run some errands and picked up a few things from the grocery store. Samantha had walked slowly and almost aimlessly between destinations in the fresh, warm day. She had soaked up the sunshine and relished the freedom from the depressing confines of the apartment. There had been no real rush anyway, other than that it was almost lunchtime and she needed to get back to fix something to eat for herself and Jason. Jason, who may or may not be off his rocker when she got there. So she had delayed for as long as she could.

The apartment door closed with a click, and Samantha kicked off her short black boots. She walked to the kitchen to put the bags down on the floor beside the island. As she did, she saw that the office door was closed. Sam paused for a moment after setting the bags down and listened. Nothing. All quiet from inside the office. He's probably napping, she thought. Perhaps for the best, she conceded.

Sam pictured Jason folded over his desk with the keyboard keys mashing into his scruffy face. She pictured herself opening the door. He would wake, looking at her groggily with hash marks implanted into his forehead and below his tired eyes. Sam shook the silly image from her mind, grabbed the wipes, and went to work wiping and putting away the items from the bags.

She ruefully wondered if they would ever go back to the old ways of living. Touching surfaces left, right, and center and not worrying about deadly microscopic death dealers. Would she someday bring things into their home without being compelled to promptly apply all her focus and attention to cleaning the potentially germ-laden intruders?

Probably not, she resigned. Those times felt so long ago, like another lifetime; someone else's memories.

Samantha thought Jason would wake up from the sounds of pans banging and utensils scraping in the kitchen. She thought the smell of salmon that now seared and hissed in the pan would beckon him like a sailor to the siren's call.

Not today.

Samantha grabbed the seared meat with metal tongs and placed a piece on both plates. She spooned out the potatoes— fried crisp on the outside but light and fluffy on the inside. Sam cut a grapefruit and set one half on each plate. She finished the dishes with powdered sugar, sprinkled gently over the grapefruit's juicy, pink flesh.

A little sweet for the sour.

She set the plates down at the usual spots on the island and paused.

"Lunch is ready!" she called. She waited for a moment. "Jay?"

Samantha walked over to the door with a sigh and opened it slowly. She called his name once more, just a decibel above a whisper.

Inside, Jason was sitting stiffly at his desk. He was staring straight ahead with a blank expression, cleaning his gun. Samantha stood quietly in the doorway, frozen in place.

The office was dark but not completely black, as the small desk lamp gave off an orange glow that mixed eerily with the computer monitor's pale white light. The strange orange light hit Jason's features in an odd way that made him look different. Sam barely recognized him. His face showed no expression, and his body showed no movement except for his arms and hands.

Francine sat cold and imposing on the desk in front of him. He was holding her barrel with his left hand and gently running his cloth over her stock with his right. Samantha looked for the box of shells but didn't see them on the desk. She felt a small pang of relief that calmed her, but only a little. Jason did not acknowledge Samantha's entry, nor did he indicate he was aware of her presence at all. He just sat, staring ahead, running his cloth in circles over Francine's smooth wooden body. Many thoughts passed through Samantha's mind. Was he angry and ignoring her? Was he sleepwalking again? Sleep-cleaning his gun, for Christ's sake?

Was he going crazy? Was she?

Sam stood paralyzed by the strange sight and her racing mind, until finally the thought of quietly backing out of the room and closing the door came to her.

That's what she did.

She stepped back once, then twice. She grasped the cool, brass handle of the door and swung it shut with a single, quiet click. Scared and confused, she stared at the door she had just closed.

She was frozen, stuck there, not knowing what to do. What else could she do? She went to the fridge and opened it.

Her hand reached out to grab the bottle of rose, but suddenly stopped. Her eyes ogled the seductive curves of the bottle longingly as her arm floated in the cold light of the refrigerator.

"Damnit," she said and closed the door.

* * *

"Did I miss lunch?" Jason said as he appeared from the office room. He looked disappointed. "About an hour ago," Samantha replied from the couch. She had her laptop open on the coffee table. "Damn," he said. "Was that it?"

Jason looked over at the cold plate of food on the island.

"Sorry, babe, I guess I fell asleep. I'll throw it in the microwave."

"You guess you fell asleep?" Samantha asked accusingly. "You don't know?"

Jason's face took on a puzzled expression as he removed the grapefruit and deposited the plate in the microwave mounted above the stove.

"Well, I dunno," he started. "After you left, I picked my sorry ass off the floor and had a quick shower. I felt pretty good and started working, getting lots done, and then..." he trailed off.

Samantha waited impatiently.

"And then?" she urged, annoyed that she had to prod him along.

"Then I dunno. Here I am."

He shot a meek smile at Sam, and he could tell she was not impressed.

"Sooo...you don't remember cleaning your gun?"

"What!?" Jason gasped. "Don't screw with me, Sam; I'm not in the mood."

"I'm not screwing around, Jay. I made lunch, and normally you come out when you hear me in the kitchen or the smell or whatever, but today you didn't. I called your name and knocked on the door, but you didn't answer, so I went in. You were sitting there like a zombie just cleaning your gun. I thought you were ignoring me or something from our fight or whatever this morning."

Samantha's words trembled as she spoke, realizing the gravity of the situation.

"You don't remember at all?"

"Goddamn sleep-cleaning my shotgun? What the fuck Sam? What am I gonna do?"

Jason's words came out rough and halted, and his voiced squeaked a little at the end.

Samantha got up, and they walked towards each other and hugged. She grabbed him hard and pressed her face into his chest. Jason winced from the pain in his shoulder, his thoughts preoccupied with the realization that he might be going crazy after all. "When's your sleep doctor appointment?"

Jason's shirt muffled Samantha's words.

"In a few days," he replied.

"Jason?"

"Yeah?"

"I'm pregnant."

CHAPTER 15

FRIDAY CAME LIKE CHRISTMAS, SLOW AND FULL OF hope and anticipation. The sleep appointment was slated for late afternoon, and Jason could think of little else. Except, perhaps, that he was going to be a dad soon. He desperately needed Dr. Luu's help. How could he be a father and look after Samantha and the baby if he was batshit?

Jason was sitting in the apartment's office, the door open today, staring blankly at his computer monitor. He had work to do but couldn't focus. And he had been getting behind lately. Jason had had a video meeting the previous day with his fearless leader, William, and it had not gone well. Jason had fallen behind, and the work he had submitted was mediocre at best.

"I know the situation isn't ideal," William had said. "But I'm counting on your big brain to deliver what I know it can deliver."

Jason had just sat there, trying not to look tired and distracted.

"Sorry William, I'll get it together, I promise."

"If you need anything, Jason, please reach out." Video meetings; the new normal.

After William had disconnected from the call, Jason had unbuttoned the top two buttons of his black dress shirt and discarded it in the corner of the room. The wifebeater under-neath was much more comfortable.

He wore that same, slightly smelly tank top today, the Friday morning of the appointment. It was like the last glim-mer of hope; the last bastion of sanity in a dark, befuddled world. Jason didn't know what he would do if Dr. Luu couldn't help him.

Perish the thought.

Dr. Luu HAD to help him. After all, Jason couldn't be the first person who moved shit around in their sleep, listened to the walls, and sleepwalked in the middle of the day, right? At the very least, the good doctor would likely prescribe some little blue or green pill to treat the symptoms.

Jesus, thought Jason, what if I need an actual therapist? Or what if I'm so fucked up that even that therapist can't do anything for me?

I'm gonna be a terrible dad.

Jason's thoughts were interrupted as Samantha darkened the doorway.

"Hey."

"Hey," he replied.

The couple just watched each other for a few moments. The laptop fan kicked on, and the sound mingled abrasively with the hum behind the walls. It was like two choir singers who couldn't quite harmonize. It set Jason's teeth on edge.

"Lunch is almost ready."

Samantha looked down and motioned to leave when Jason said, "Thanks, babe."

She stopped and looked back into his eyes. They were tired but kind, softened by thoughts of the day ahead.

"You're a saint for putting up with this, with me. I know

it's hard, but you are still there for me, for us. God, it's corny, but you are my rock, you know, my lighthouse. You guide the way. I will get better for you, Sam. For you and the baby."

His eyes moved from hers to her stomach. A little pang of fear gripped his insides. It was the first time he mentioned the baby directly to Samantha. When she broke the news two days ago, he had simply hugged her tight and whispered in her ear, "It's going to be ok."

Samantha's smile was kind and soft as she stepped towards Jason to ruffle his scruffy hair. She brushed it to the side, and its natural oils kept it in place.

"I love you," she said and kissed his forehead. Samantha turned and left for the kitchen, leaving Jason sitting at his desk, looking out the now empty doorway.

* * *

"Drive safe," Sam said as Jason stood at the apartment door.

"Thanks," he replied. "I don't know how long it will be. The receptionist said it's just a consultation today, so we'll see. You'll prolly be back from your thing before me."

Samantha nodded. She had an ultrasound appointment three blocks away, but not for another hour. It was the final step in the 'am I really pregnant' process. Blood and urine can give false positives, but there's no denying the picture up on that screen—it's either there or it's not.

Jason rode the elevator down to the parking garage. He exited the lift and headed towards the black SUV. Another person was getting into their car a few stalls over, and their door shut with an echo that bounced off the grey concrete walls.

Jason's footsteps also echoed as he pulled out the key

fob to unlock his vehicle. The locks opened with a whir and a click, and he opened the door and got in. While pushing in the brake and ignition button to start the car, Jason wondered how long it had been since he last drove. Almost a week, he figured. It was strange to go from driving every day to barely driving at all.

Jason pulled out of his parking spot, mentally calculating how much money they had saved on gas in the last three months. Driving felt foreign, and Jason was awkward behind the wheel until the large metal gate pulled up and open and he entered the street.

There were more vehicles on the street now than at the beginning of the pandemic. However, there were still noticeably fewer than before the lockdown. Usually, a typical Friday afternoon in the city would be quite busy, but with nowhere to go and thousands of people now out of work, Jason was at the sleep clinic twenty minutes early. He pulled into the lot and parked in a spot that faced the front of the building. It was a standalone three-story building, quite old, with brown bricks, a flat roof, and several large, single-pane windows. There was no big sign announcing the building's occupant, just letters on the door's window: Dr. Luu, sleep therapist.

Jason pulled out his phone, typed in his password, and opened his conversation with Samantha.

"Here now, a little early," he wrote.

The ellipses appeared beside her name to indicate she was typing.

"Ok. Good luck!" Samantha's words appeared on the screen, followed by a thumbs-up emoji.

Jason took a breath, put his phone in his pocket, slipped his surgical mask over his mouth and nose, and went inside.

The front door that Jason entered through opened into a lobby waiting area. He was a bit surprised at how new and clean the inside looked compared to the outside of the building. The old building's main floor seemed to have recently been renovated into what looked like a regular doctor's office.

Red plastic chairs with low backs were spaced apart on the glossy black and white checkerboard linoleum floor tiles. A red leather couch rested against a side wall with a Ficus tree standing guard beside it. Jason's footsteps rang loudly as he walked past an older woman and a child on his way towards the reception desk.

The boy looked ragged, dressed in cheap hand-me-downs and a newsie hat, like he had been transported from the dirty thirties. His pale face and sunken eyes followed Jason as he passed. The boy's mother reached down and put a protective arm around the child. She did not make eye contact, but Jason noted that she looked just as tired as the boy.

There was something else, though.

Behind the tired, wrinkled face was fear. Jason could sense it right away; how she grabbed the kid and recoiled from Jason's presence. Even though she wasn't looking at him, Jason saw the fear in those eyes.

Maybe the kid was delivering newspapers in his sleep, Jason mused.

Normally he would smile to himself after a joke like that, but the child and his mother were so pathetic-looking that it seemed cruel.

Hopefully they get the help they need, he amended internally.

"Good day, can I help you?" The receptionist was an older lady with grey curls cut short. Jason wondered if there was a specific age when women cut their hair short or if it was more of a feeling they got rather than a hard-and-fast rule. She looked at him through the plexiglass with sharp blue eyes. A white surgical mask covered her face, while a white, knitted sweater covered her bright red scrubs.

"I have an appointment at four with Dr. Luu?"

More of a question than a statement. "Jason Steele," he added after noting she would likely need his name. "Dr. Luu will be with you shortly, please have a seat."

The receptionist's voice was high-pitched and nasal, and it sounded far away through the holes in the plexiglass.

Jason nodded, said thank you, and sat down on a chair near the Ficus—on the opposite side of the room from the boy and his mother.

As Jason sat down, he looked up to see the lady looking at him now. She stared at him with her beady black eyes and hard face while clasping the boy close. Her black mask covered most of her face, but Jason pictured a big, witchy nose and a snarling mouth, half filled with decaying teeth. Probably unfair, but he didn't like how she was looking at him. She held his gaze until Jason started feeling uncomfortable and looked away. He pulled his phone out as people do when bored, needing to look busy, socially awkward, or scared of human interaction. It was the latter for Jason currently. He definitely did not want to interact with those two.

"Sir?" said the nasal voice from far away. "Sir, you can't have your phone out in here. Sorry. It's for privacy concerns. Thank you."

The steely blue eyes penetrated the plexiglass all the way through to Jason's nerves. They gave him the willies. "Oh, sorry," he said as he dumbly noticed the several signs on the wall showing a picture of a cell phone with a line through it. He deposited the phone back in his pocket and sat back.

The red plastic chairs were remarkably comfortable, as if made for his exact ass shape. There was no tv on the wall and no magazines. He couldn't use his phone and hadn't brought a book. The woman was still observing Jason with an offending glare. There was only one thing left to do—close his eyes and try to relax.

Green blurred all around Jason as he ran. The thin brown path ran under his feet like a dirt treadmill. Jason ran and ran. He gasped for breath, and his lungs burned and wheezed.

On and on the forest passed as he sprinted. His muscles screamed from the exertion as his heart pounded blood through his veins. His face was calm though, almost serene. His dark-blue eyes were fixed on the path ahead. He knew what he was looking for, and he was on the right track.

Up ahead, in a small clearing, his eyes found the prize, splayed out amongst the dirt, rocks, and dead leaves. The deer had run out the last of its strength and collapsed here, succumbing to its injury. The bullet hole oozed dark crimson, which was beginning to pool on the ground.

The young doe struggled to breathe; snot and steam poured from her nostrils while her tongue hung limp and lifeless from her mouth. Jason approached her, and she didn't have the energy to escape. She simply lay there with one terror-stricken eye staring up at him.

Where had he seen that before?

Jason bent over with his rifle in one hand, looking down, into the eye.

Where had he seen that before?

So familiar.

He watched with morbid fascination as she struggled to hold on to life. The pool of blood grew and grew and started to swirl. The swirl hypnotized Jason. He stared, his face expressionless and dumb. He felt cold and weak, and his rifle fell to the ground.

"Jason!" shouted a familiar voice from far away behind him. "JASON!" Was that Samantha?

"SAM!" he screamed.

He drew a deep breath, and his bloodshot eyes refocused on the pool of blood that continued to swirl. But the swirling pool was no longer fed from the hole in the deer; it was flowing from the front of a woman; the hiker. The liquid was pouring from so many holes, like a dozen bloody streams feeding a red lake of death.

Jason recoiled in horror.

"Oh God, what the fu…"

He fell back onto his tailbone, sending a shooting pain into his skull.

"No, no, no…"

His eyes slowly made their way up her bloodied torso to her face. He was terrified of what he would see, but he couldn't stop himself. Finally, past the pale, sunken cheeks and blue lips, his eyes locked with hers. Dull and deep, her eyes locked him in and wouldn't let go. Jason stared, breathing sharp, deep, and labored breaths.

Into the abyss.

He felt it call to him, beckoning. It seemed…peaceful. Even the cold nothingness would be better than this hell.

He succumbed.

Jason's taut muscles relaxed, his breathing slowed, the beads of sweat dried on his brow, and he fell in.

CHAPTER 16

"**J**ASON." THE NAME SEEMED FAMILIAR.

"Jason?" The voice was echoey and distant but soon drew nearer. Jason opened his eyes to the bright lights of the sleep clinic waiting room. Realization dawned on his face and he took in a deep breath—the kind you take after holding your breath underwater for some time—and straightened himself up in the plastic red chair. Cobwebs and faint memories of a forgotten dream cleared from his mind as a short man in a white lab coat stood over him.

"You should save that for the tests, Jason."

Dr. Luu's eyes squinted against the raised cheeks of the smile that hid behind his mask.

"All is well?" the doctor asked.

"Yes, sorry. Nodded off there," Jason said, mildly embarrassed.

"Happens all the time, not to worry. Now, please join me in my office."

Dr. Luu turned and headed towards the door beside the receptionist's desk. Jason shook his head slightly and stood up. The woman and the child were gone. He wondered how long he had been asleep.

As the two men entered Dr. Luu's office, the doctor gestured for Jason to sit and closed the door. The checkered tiles clicked as their footsteps fell. The room was bright and minimalist. In the middle of the room was a chrome-legged desk with a white top. Two chrome-legged chairs faced the desk. The seats were black, not red as Jason half expected. He took a seat in the one on his right. Dr. Luu went around the desk and sat down in his modern, ergonomic, high-backed chair. He wiggled the mouse to wake up his sleeping computer. It came alive with a flicker of the screen. Jason rubbed his palms on his knees as he sat, looking around the sterile-looking room.

The walls were a crisp white; its only adornments several diplomas and awards.

Dr. Luu looked up at Jason and then at the framed documents on the wall beside him.

"Oh, those? Those are to hopefully put you at ease more than an obvious boast about me," he chuckled. Jason allowed himself to relax into the chair. The diplomas and accolades did help after all; good to know this doctor wasn't some quack.

Dr. Luu typed for a moment, then looked from the screen to Jason.

Slipping on his clear-rimmed glasses, Dr. Luu observed his new patient.

"You look tired."

Jason noticed that he didn't feel insulted, likely because a doctor had said it. Dr. Luu had an accent, but his English was excellent, and he spoke loudly and with purpose through the white surgical mask.

Jason fumbled with how to begin. So much had happened in the last three months. Enough to fill three years, he thought. His time in Seattle seemed to have crept along, deadly slow and mundane until sporadic sparks of insanity woke him from his slumber. Yet the three months had also passed so quickly.

In what seemed like an instant, he had gone from starting a new, exciting life to sitting in a cold, bright doctor's office trying to explain how fucked up he was. He shook his head.

"It's ok, Jason," the doctor said, obviously aware of Jason's struggle to find the right words. "Just start where you can."

"Truth is, Doc; it's hard to know where to start. I mean, when I moved in with Sam—that's my girlfriend—three years ago or whatever, she brought up that I talked in my sleep. She said that I sometimes moved around a bit; like I elbowed her once, all herky-jerky in my sleep. It came up in conversation with my dad, and he said I'd been doing that since I was a kid. Nothing to worry about."

Jason paused, cleared his throat, and then continued.

"Dad said he does it, and his dad did it before him. I didn't think about it much. And it didn't seem to bother Sam, before."

Dr. Luu quietly typed as Jason spoke.

"Then we moved here, and I dunno. It got worse. Like a lot worse."

Jason's pace quickened.

"I move stuff in my sleep. All the stuff on top of my nightstand ends up inside my nightstand. Oh, and I sleepwalk now, I guess. Sometimes I wake up on the floor in the bedroom or the bathroom. And I don't remember how I got there."

Jason stared at his hands as he described the time he fell asleep in his office in the middle of the day and then woke up, mid sleepwalk, to see Samantha staring at him with fear in her eyes. Jason paused, then opened his mouth as if to speak again and stopped. He decided to omit the most recent disturbance during which he had apparently sleep-cleaned his gun. That was not something Jason was ready to accept or discuss. He wasn't sure how the good doctor might react. He might label him insane on the spot and in need of padded walls.

"She said I do it all the time now. She says I stand beside the wall with my ear up against it, listening, I guess."

Dr. Luu stopped typing.

"Listening?"

Jason looked up at the doctor and then away, embarrassed. His cheeks flushed and tiny beads of sweat began to form on his forehead. His beard felt itchy and dry.

"Well, listening, I guess. To the hum."

Dr. Luu listened intently while Jason spoke. He touched on his relationship with his father and how his mother left them when he was a child. He discussed the stress of moving. The new job, new apartment, new city, and the fear and unknown of the pandemic. Jason went on about the stifling lockdown and its negative effect on his relationship with Samantha.

He told the doctor how they had wanted to get away to explore some of the beautiful scenery Washington state had to offer. And how they had happened upon a waking nightmare when they all but witnessed the murder of that poor hiker up in the mountains.

He described the gnawing, relentless hum as if it were something alive. Something that knew its own evil nature and basked in the triumph of its exquisite torture.

The doctor interjected here and there to ask a question but mostly let Jason vomit words all over the office. Dr. Luu's fingers tapped frantically on the keyboard to capture the words and record them on the screen.

Jason finally finished. He realized he was now sitting on the edge of his chair, leaning forward. His breathing was labored and shallow as if he had just run the quarter mile. Jason shot the doctor a meek smile and relaxed back into his chair. The muscles around his lungs relaxed, and he took in a deep, calming breath.

"Wow," he said. "Seems like a lot when you put it all out there, huh?"

Dr. Luu finished his notes and looked over at Jason, observing the young man silently.

"It actually feels…pretty good to get that off my chest, Doc. Damn! It's like the foot that's been standing on my throat has eased off the pressure a bit." Jason rubbed the back of his head as he spoke.

Dr. Luu sat quietly a moment longer. The room was silent as he thoughtfully watched Jason.

"There is a lot to unpack here, Jason," he began. "Thank you for coming in and trusting me enough to share your experiences. There is no doubt that stress is a major factor affecting your sleep right now, but I would like to run some tests to find out more. I do have a room available tomorrow night if you would like to come back and spend the night?"

Dr. Luu's eyebrows raised with his voice as he asked the question.

"Whatever I gotta do, Doc. I just want to get better, I…I feel like I'm going nuts over here."

"You aren't going nuts, Jason," Dr. Luu said with a slight smile, "but you are under a great amount of stress. We will see what the tests say and go from there. How does that sound?"

"Sounds like hope," Jason said, semi-sardonically. He wanted to hope, but he didn't know if he could fully allow it.

"Good. Here is some information for you, along with

some instructions to follow before your appointment. Please look it over when you get home."

Dr. Luu opened a drawer in his desk, took out a folder, and handed it to Jason as they both got up. "Oh, uh…hey Doc," Jason stammered. "You think you could give me something, you know, to help me sleep better tonight?"

There was that feeling again: hope, hope that the good doctor had some blue liquid gels laying around somewhere that he could kindly gift to Jason.

"I'm sorry, Jason," Dr. Luu said, "You must not change anything about your sleep routine. Don't take anything you don't normally take. No sleeping pills. Not even a chamomile tea or hot bath if that's not your normal routine, ok?"

Jason nodded dejectedly.

"Once we run some tests and talk a bit more, we can see if a sleep aid is necessary."

"Thank you kindly, Doc. I look forward to seeing you tomorrow then."

Dr. Luu bowed his head slightly, and Jason turned and left the office. He walked through the door, into the waiting room, and across its black and white checkered floor. Jason's thoughts dwelled on the possibility that this man might make him better. He allowed his feelings to swell into hopefulness. As Jason pushed open the metal door into the cool, crisp evening and took in a sharp breath of air, he felt relief. He was so distracted by the alien feeling that he didn't notice the woman and child staring at him from the window above.

CHAPTER 17

JASON QUICKLY TEXTED SAMANTHA TO LET HER KNOW that he was on his way and pulled out onto the street. It was dark, so he had put on his prescription glasses. The way the headlights and streetlamps mingled and bounced off the city's glass and concrete caused a distracting glare. Jason wasn't required to wear glasses when driving, his eyes weren't that bad, but the thin-rimmed glasses sharpened images at a distance, which helped put him at ease.

Driving was a stressful thing—gasoline-filled chunks of heavy metal and rubber, barreling down the road, guided only by people and their limited attention spans. They were basically driving ticking time bombs that were waiting to go off.

About four years prior, not long before Jason had met Samantha, some dummy had run a stop sign, causing Jason to T-bone the shiny new Cadillac. Luckily this happened on a back street, and the vehicles collided at only about thirty miles per hour. Not enough to kill you, really, but enough to injure or at least shake you up. Especially if you weren't wearing a seatbelt, which Jason wasn't.

His body had bounced off the airbag with a flash of powder and pain. He had sat dazed as his car began to smoke, disabled in the intersection. Playing repeatedly in Jason's mind was the image of the fellow in the passenger seat seeing Jason's car coming and instantly recognizing the danger, their eyes meeting. Eyes filled with fear, like a dying deer. Like the dead hiker. All in a flash. The poor guy probably shit himself.

It had been a hot July day, so the passenger's window was down. Good thing, or he would have cracked his head wide open right there and maybe died.

Jason's daze had turned to concern as he checked his body for injuries and checked it again.

He had gotten out, walked over to the curb, and sat down. The ambulance sirens had wailed in the distance as Jason watched the driver get out, hurry to the passenger side of what used to be his shiny, new Cadillac, and swore. He swore, and he swore again, inspecting the crumpled steel and chipped paint where his door used to be. The driver stomped his foot like some angry child. He noticed Jason sitting on the curb from the corner of his eye.

"Hey man, you ok?" he asked.

Jason said that he was.

The driver's face then turned red and flushed. He took a step towards Jason.

"You should watch where the fuck you're going, man! You almost killed us!" The driver's words shook Jason from his quiet stupor. His eyes focused on the angry man and narrowed into slits.

Jason stood up, causing the Cadillac driver to take a step back.

"Are you kidding me?" Jason roared. "You ran a fucking stop sign, you dumb, stupid fuck!"

The man's angry face had flushed with embarrassment as he followed Jason's pointed finger to the bright red octagon standing on the corner. The driver of the Cadillac stood there in shock.

"I didn't even see it, man. I didn't even see it."

When the ambulance finally arrived, one paramedic came over and asked if Jason was alright or needed to go to the hospital. Jason said he was fine, just a little shaken up. He had surveyed his body and felt no cracked ribs from the collision with the airbag; no severe pain in his neck or head from the sudden stop. He just felt like he had taken a good ass-kicking.

He had given his statement to the police as he watched the paramedics tend to the passenger, whose look of realization and fear would forever be etched into Jason's memory. The paramedics braced the passenger's broken right arm and tied it to his body. His face contorted, and he let out quick bursts of angry pain as they moved him from the front seat onto a stretcher.

Insurance had paid for Jason's car; not that it was worth much. Jason had considered suing the guy. He had visions of himself showing up in court with some greasy lawyer and a thick, white brace wrapped around his neck. But when he attended court as a summoned witness for the state, he found out that the driver—Micky Johns—had had a few afternoon pops that day and blew over on the breathalyzer. And apparently, this wasn't the first time either.

Micky Johns was quickly found guilty of driving under the influence, careless driving causing bodily harm, failing to obey a traffic sign, and speeding. His buddy, the passenger, had a broken right arm and cracked pelvis for his trouble. Jason's thoughts of suing this guy for everything he was worth quickly vanished as he realized the guy wasn't worth very much at all. Jason had to resign himself to being grateful that he had emerged alive and relatively unscathed.

Relatively, of course, because he did have terrible dreams

for some time after the accident. Almost every night, Jason would dream about standing on a tall, brown brick building. He would look off the edge and take a step, knowing he could fly. Except Jason couldn't fly. Everything around him would turn dark as he fell, the wind howling past his ears. The ground would rush up to meet him, but he always awoke with a jolt, right at the moment of impact.

Those dreams had eventually subsided as time passed, and the trauma of the accident softened into memory.

Jason adjusted his glasses as the SUV came to a stop. He looked left and right. His was the only vehicle at the four-way stop, so he pulled away. A few drops of rain hit the wind-shield, and he absentmindedly wiped them clean with a click of a lever.

CHAPTER 18

It began to rain harder as Jason pulled off the street into the parking garage under his apartment. The steel gate reacted to its programming and rolled into the ceiling with the sound of metal on metal. Jason brought his left arm holding the key fob back inside the SUV and closed the window. A few straggling drops of rain darkened the sleeve of his jacket where they fell. Once the metal barrier was lifted far enough out of the way, Jason pulled forward and parked the car.

The elevator stopped at the lobby, and the door opened. Jason peered out from the shiny lift to see a man peering back. He was tall and lanky, well dressed in a black suit, clean dress shoes, and a light-grey trench coat that stopped mid-leg. Jason and the well-dressed man stared at each other for a moment. "Feel free to come in if you're comfortable,"

Jason said, his blue surgical mask muffling his words slightly.

The well-dressed man's head cocked. He, too, was wearing a mask, though it was dyed black and made of cloth. It matched his jet-black hair that peaked out heavily from under his tilted fedora.

"As long as you don't mind?" the man replied as he stepped into the elevator.

They stood as far away from each other as they could.

"What floor?" Jason asked.

"Twentieth, please."

The well-dressed man had an accent that Jason couldn't quite place. Northern Michigan, he guessed, or Wisconsin. Hell, maybe the guy was some beaver-eating Canadian. Jason pushed the button, and it glowed.

"That's one floor below us," Jason said as he stared at a sign that read COVID-19 PROTOCOL: 2 PERSON MAX. OCCUPANCY with a picture of a surgical mask underneath.

The well-dressed man said nothing, only shifted. With a flash of inspiration, Jason added, "That noise must really bug you guys on the twentieth, huh?" The man turned his head to look at Jason.

"Noise?"

"Yeah," Jason continued, "you know, the mechanical room or whatever. I think Chester said it was on your floor. It sure is loud up in our place. You can hear it through the walls and everything."

The man shifted back to continue staring at the smooth, silver doors of the elevator.

"I don't hear any noise." He paused for a moment and added, "Except the neighbors' screaming kid sometimes." He chuckled to himself softly.

"Oh," said Jason quietly, "well…"

The elevator slowed and stopped at twenty. The chrome sliding doors opened with a ding. "Goodnight," the well-dressed man said and tipped his fedora before leaving the elevator. Jason stared after him, deep in thought.

The elevator dinged once more, and the door closed. Jason stared at the glowing button that read twenty-one as the gentle pull of the elevator carried him to his level.

The door opened with a ding.

Jason stared out into the hall. After a moment, the elevator let out another chime, and the door closed. Jason stared at the control panel. The elevator remained suspended in the air on the twenty-first floor. Finally, Jason pushed the button he was staring at, and the elevator descended. The car stopped again, and with a ding, the shiny doors opened.

Jason stepped out onto floor twenty.

It felt weird and alien to be on a floor that wasn't his. Uncomfortable and out of place. It was his building; he lived only one floor up, but walking around on a different floor felt odd, even though it looked the same. He walked in the direction that the well-dressed man had taken. As he passed each door, Jason observed them carefully, looking for a sign that said electrical room, or mechanical room, or even janitor closet. He found nothing but apartment numbers and a stairway. At the end of the hallway, he turned around to check the other side of the floor.

Jason walked along at a brisk pace, feeling a bit like an intruder, picturing where his place was, one floor above. Jason figured his apartment was on the other side of the building, the opposite side of the well-dressed man's place. That's why he didn't hear the hum, Jason reasoned, he's all the way over on the other side. That knowledge slightly put his mind at ease as he passed the elevator and headed for the other side; the side that his apartment was on. The side where Chester had said the mechanical room was or must be if it's not on the opposite side. Jason counted the numbers as he passed the doors. Then a stairwell. Then, Jason stopped and stared at the door at the end of the hall. The last door, the one that he expected to show *mechanical room* embossed on its little brass sign, was just like the others, except it read 2012.

Jason's brain was trying to make sense of it all. Had he heard Chester wrong? Didn't he say there was a mechanical room below their apartment? Yes, he did. He even said they had it inspected, and that everything was normal and well within the appropriate decibel level.

Well, where the hell was it then!?

Jason's thoughts raced as he stared at apartment 2012. Maybe he had missed it. He turned on his heel and swiftly rechecked all the doors on floor twenty. He had not missed it. There was nothing but apartments and stairs. As Jason pressed the elevator button to call the lift, he stood thinking, deep in thought. Maybe Chester didn't mean directly below their apartment? Perhaps a few floors down? Maybe the damn room was in the basement, but the hum traveled easily up the damn hollow walls.

And what was he going to do anyway when he found the door? Kick it? Flip it the bird?

No, he thought.

He wanted to press his ear up against it, to listen to the source.

Suddenly, the elevator dinged as the door opened. Jason gave his head a quick shake, attempting to clear it, and stepped in.

CHAPTER 19

J ASON OPENED THE APARTMENT DOOR, AND THE aroma hit him like a wave. Garlic and butter and cream filled his nostrils, and he inhaled deeply. He stepped into the apartment and closed the door behind him. Samantha was playing music on her Bluetooth speaker; some new Top 40 song that you could shake your ass to. She must be in a good mood, he thought. He kicked off his shoes, hung his jacket in the closet, and rounded the corner into the kitchen.

The room was bright and busy. The garlic cream sauce bubbled on the stove. The oven light was on, and Jason was now able to match the delicious smell of roast chicken to its source. A pot of water was waiting at a rolling boil, eager to soften the dried noodles.

Samantha was indeed shaking her ass. She was half bent over the sink, washing some of the dishes used for cooking, her round bottom swaying to the beat. Jason didn't think she'd heard him come in, so he snuck up behind her.

"Ah!" She seemed to jump about a foot in the air when Jason grabbed a firm butt cheek in each hand. She spun around in a frenzy of shock and bubbles. Foam shot across Jason's chest like he was washing cars at some high school fundraiser. His face was bright and smiling; eyes clear and mischievous.

"Jesus Christ, Jason!" Sam gasped as she held her chest with one hand. "You almost gave me a coronary!"

She leaned against the counter, her breath coming in short, sharp breaths.

Jason chuckled.

"Sorry babe, you ok?"

Smiling, he picked up a wooden spoon and began to stir the thick, white sauce.

"You bastard," she said as she turned the music down. "Now get out of here. Did you even wash your hands?"

Jason tapped the spoon and put it down. He leaned into Sam, and they kissed long and deep. She pulled her head back to see into his eyes.

"You look good. Did you have a nap over there or something?"

Jason gave her red lips a quick peck before letting her go. He walked to the sink to wash his hands.

"It was good. Like, really good. Kinda like a therapy session or something. I just talked and talked, and the doctor just listened and took notes. Felt good to get some of that shit off my chest, Sam."

He finished rinsing and turned off the tap. Samantha handed him the towel from the front of the oven. "Thanks," he said as he dried his hands.

"Well?" Samantha asked expectantly, "what did he say?"

"Nothing much."

Sam's expression turned curious.

"He just said I have a lot to unpack, whatever that means, but that I'm to go back tomorrow night and sleep over. I guess they're gonna strap some probes to my head and see what happens. "Polysomnography," Sam said.

"Huh?"

"It's the test they use to diagnose sleep disorders. I googled it today. The page is still open on the laptop if you want to look it over before your test tomorrow."

Jason cocked an eyebrow.

"Yeah, I guess I should, huh."

Samantha turned and poured the dried noodles into the boiling water.

"I started dinner when you texted me. I almost had the timing right, but I didn't want to overcook the noodles. Good thing you took a little longer than I expected."

Sam stirred the noodles to prevent them from sticking while Jason thought about his discovery on the twentieth floor.

"Thank you. Smells good," he said, opting not to fill her in.

* * *

"It will be the first night I'll spend alone since we got here."

Samantha stuck her stainless-steel fork through the soft penne. She moved the noodles around in the creamy sauce and brought the fork up and into her mouth.

"You gonna be ok here all by yourself?"

"I suppose," she said after she finished chewing.

"At least you'll get the whole bed to yourself." Samantha nodded.

"Sure. Big ol' empty bed to match the big ol' empty apartment."

"It's not that big," Jason said.

"Actually, it's fucking tiny." They laughed together.

"But still," Sam continued, "It's lonely here. I don't know anyone; this pandemic has stopped me from meeting anyone or finding a job or doing anything really. I just sit around, mostly bored, not knowing how you are from moment to moment."

Jason frowned.

"I know, babe." Jason put his fork down. "I'm sorry things have been so crazy. But I have a really good feeling about this doctor. I think he's gonna get to the bottom of this thing so I can get better."

Jason's face looked hopeful and flushed as he spoke, staring into Sam's dark eyes.

"I will get better, Sam. I love you."

"I love you too."

Jason leaned in to kiss her and their mouths parted. Samantha reached out her hands for Jason's face. She pulled his lips tighter against hers by the scruff of his beard, and she let out a little moan. Heat rushed to Jason's groin at the sound of her pleasure. He ran his left hand through her shiny, obsidian hair and grabbed tight, pulling just enough for her to feel it. Her eyes rolled back into her head, and their tongues danced wildly in each other's mouths. Jason's free hand reached up and out and found Samantha's firm, full breast. Her flesh gave way to his passionate squeeze; her nipple hardened and poked at his palm. His thumb and forefinger collapsed around the eager hardness, and he pinched just enough for a little pain. Samantha squealed. Jason stood up off of his stool and pulled her off hers. Still kissing, she grabbed him close, pressing his throbbing manhood against her stomach. She jumped up and clasped her legs around his waist, wordlessly begging Jason to take her to the bedroom.

He eagerly obliged, carrying his lover across the apartment floor and onto the bed.

* * *

From the bathroom came the steady hiss of the shower mixed with music from Samantha's Bluetooth speaker. Jason lay in bed, glistening with sweat, catching his breath, listening.

Sam started to sing along to a song. She had a beautiful voice. One that wasn't forced or fake. Just a wholesome, clear voice. She loved music. She had been in a choir back home (would this ever feel like home?) and even took piano lessons before leaving Pennsylvania. She had had every intention to join a new choir out here and to begin lessons again.

COVID had other plans, Jason thought, staring up at the ceiling. Samantha loved that speaker. She loved that speaker because it allowed her to take her music anywhere. Sam would sleep with it if she could. Samantha used to, before Jason, but Jason can't fall asleep when music was playing. Too distracting, he had said. He would sing along in his head or out loud for hours until exhaustion finally took him. Sam had suggested he try again to block out the hum of their new apartment. He tried it, of course. Anything to drown out the hum.

It had been no good, though. He had ended up just singing along.

Jason had tried everything; the Bluetooth speaker playing music, and headphones playing soft nature sounds that promised sleep would be achieved in only minutes. Some other offerings used hypnosis to lull you to sleep. Jason didn't like the idea of being programmed, so he had vetoed that idea. He had also tried earplugs, but he couldn't get comfortable with them in. They blocked the air in and put pressure on his eardrums, making his head feel full and heavy.

The only thing that worked, a little, was running a fan. The fan created a white noise that hid the hum just enough that Jason wouldn't focus on it so much. The hum hadn't gone away, though; it was ever-present. Constant and relentless, like a freight train. The fan would sometimes distract him long enough to fall asleep, but mostly he would lie there, *feeling* the hum through the fan's white noise. The vibration would tickle at his insides at first, then grow louder as it moved into his ears. Louder and louder, up, into his mind, into a great crescendo!

Then he would wake up somewhere and not know how he got there, or discover he had moved things, or his body would ache as if he had been lifting weights or jogging in his sleep.

The gentle sound of the shower mixed with some slow jam playing on the speaker continued. Samantha was humming along; what a pleasant sound. Not like the other one, no, this hum was nice and soft and warm.

Jason rolled his head over and looked at the nightstand. Below his lamp lay all the things that liked to move around at night, gathered around the lamp like they were relaxing under a tree on a warm, summer day. Fuck it, he thought. Move around if you want; I don't care anymore. His heavy eyelids blinked lazily and finally closed, Samantha's sweet hum in his mind.

* * *

Jason blinked again. The room was bright. He squinted against the light and rolled over. Samantha was lying beside him. As his eyes rested upon her face, she opened her eyes, shards of obsidian staring back at him.

"Good morning," she said as she cozied into her pillow. Jason stared a moment.

"Hey there."

Jason yawned and stretched, kicking the comforter off his right leg.

"Damn! I guess I passed out hard, huh?" he said, lying on his back.

Samantha inched closer, ran her hand along his naked torso, and rested it on his chest, running her fingernails through his short chest hair.

"You were out cold when I came to bed. You looked so peaceful."

Samantha smiled and cozied in closer to Jason. He looked over at his nightstand, expecting to have to fish everything out of the drawer again. Instead, everything was exactly where it had been the night before—lying under the lamp-tree, taking shade from the hot, summer sun.

"I haven't slept that well in forever!" Jason reached over, put his arm around Sam, and hugged her tight. "I guess talking to the doctor really did help," Sam said.

Jason kissed her cheek.

"I definitely felt lighter after the appointment. It took the edge off, I guess. Looking forward to tonight. Hopefully we can learn something." Jason's eyes were clear and bright, and his dimples showed through his beard.

"You hungry?"

* * *

"Chef Jason's famous French toast!" Jason announced as he lifted the golden-brown bread from the pan onto their plates.

"Mmm!" Samantha exclaimed as she took a sip of orange juice. Jason's mouth watered from the aroma of toasted wheat and egg mixed with vanilla and cinnamon.

He sat down, and they dug in.

CHAPTER 20

"**G**OT EVERYTHING?" SAMANTHA ASKED. JASON checked over his bag and took a mental inventory. The day had moved slowly for the couple as they waited in anticipation for the night to come. The all-important test on which so much depended. They had watched some tv after breakfast. It had been more of the same—huge numbers of infected, disturbing numbers dead, no vaccine in sight. The president promised late fall, but most critics said that was impossible. Once they got their morbid fill, the couple decided to get some air.

They waved to Chester as they passed the concierge desk. He seemed to be training another new concierge. Samantha and Jason exited the doors and headed out onto the street. It was cool but pleasant outside, with a light, briny breeze coming in off the harbor. They strolled down to the seawall and across the section where the speeding cyclist had struck Jason. Jason rubbed his shoulder absentmindedly and called the cyclist a blind twit as the couple discussed what had happened that day.

No one's fault, really. Just bad luck.

They continued down the walkway, wandering through the city in a wide loop. Building after building was closed and shuttered. After about an hour, they arrived back near their apartment. They stopped at one of the restaurants that had reopened for takeout and delivery only. Jason asked for two orders of fish and chips through the intercom at the front window. The masked person inside wrote down the order with gloved hands and then replied, "It'll be about ten minutes."

After fifteen minutes, the couple received their order and hurried back to their apartment, leaving a mouth-watering trail of deep-fried food aromas in their wake.

Jason commented, as he did every time they ate fish out west that, "They just couldn't get fresh fish like this back home."

The afternoon consisted of more tv, some sudoku, and researching sleep disorders on the internet. The day crawled by as Jason checked the time every ten minutes or so, a pattern that was broken up by dinner and packing. At 8:30 p.m., Jason stood in front of Samantha.

"Ready to go?" she asked.

"I think so," Jason said as he looked into Sam's sad but hopeful eyes.

"You gonna be ok here all alone?"

"I think so," Samantha said.

They smiled, and Jason grabbed her waist and pulled her close.

"I'll text you later if I can."

He kissed her cheek, grabbed his duffle, and opened the apartment door.

"Love you," he said as he paused and looked back. "Ditto."

* * *

It was dark and the sky was clear when Jason pulled his SUV out into the street. He looked up through his glasses and sunroof and thought he saw a few faded stars behind the city's light pollution. Jason turned the radio on with a push of a button, and Bob Marley started singing from the speakers, telling Jason not to worry about a thing.

"If you say so, Bob. You're the boss!"

Jason tapped along to the music and smiled while driving happily over to the sleep clinic.

He pulled into the same spot he had the previous day and shifted into park. There were several other cars there, and as Jason looked up the old building's brown brick walls, he wondered how many sleep test rooms there were inside.

Three floors, he thought. The main floor is the waiting room and offices, and the second and third floors were the test rooms maybe. Four rooms per floor. Eight rooms? He would soon find out. But why hadn't he gone in yet?

He remained sitting in his car, staring up at the building; bright lights shone from the windows on the second and third floors. Jason suddenly had a terrible thought—what if the test shows something is really wrong in my head? What if my brain is so fucked up, I'll be doing weird shit in my sleep for the rest of my life? Would Sam even put up with that?

His thoughts quickened.

What if they find a tumor or cancer or something in there? What if I'm dying and going crazy along the way?

Jason shifted in his seat as he stared at the entrance.

Or, he thought somberly, what if they find nothing at all? What if good ol' Doctor Luu can't find anything wrong at all. That would be worse, wouldn't it? Jason sat a minute longer, blank faced and statuesque. Finally, the realization that he would be late sparked his body to move.

Almost automatically, he grabbed his phone and wallet

from the middle console, his duffle from the passenger seat, and went inside.

"Good evening Mr. Steele," the receptionist greeted. She eyed him as his shoes clicked on the black and white linoleum.

"Hello."

"Nine o'clock appointment, is it?"

Jason nodded. "Yes, that's correct."

He scanned the waiting room, thinking he might see the strange boy and haggard woman staring at him again. He did not.

"I'll have you fill out this questionnaire and sign a waiver before we head up, please."

The receptionist handed Jason a clipboard from her chair behind the desk.

"A waiver, huh?" Jason joked, "should I be worried?"

His hidden smile faded against her lack of humor. The receptionist simply held the clipboard out with a flat, emotionless expression. Jason cleared his throat, nodded, and took the board.

Once Jason had answered the questions and signed the waiver, the receptionist led him up the stairs to the second floor. Long hardwood boards passed underfoot as they walked down the corridor. The first door on the left was closed. Jason peered into the first room on his right. It wasn't nosiness; at least, not entirely. There is a certain natural tendency to look in a doorway as one passes.

In his mind, leading up to his appointment, Jason had pictured the sleep clinic test rooms similar to hospital rooms. He expected hospital beds with sterile white sheets and stainless-steel instruments sitting on stainless-steel trays. He pictured it all under cold fluorescent lights with the smell of antiseptic in the air.

Instead, the room he saw as he passed was very much like a regular bedroom. It was warm and inviting, illuminated by soft, yellow light. A cozy bed with a headboard was against the wall, and a boy was lying under the brown and forest green blankets. The boy's face turned to the door as Jason passed. Their tired eyes met briefly. It sent a shiver down Jason's spine.

Was that the same boy from yesterday? he wondered. It was hard to tell without the old school clothes and the odd lady who had hovered over the boy before. The receptionist's voice broke through Jason's thoughts.

"On the right, Mr. Steele."

Jason shook the thoughts from his head and turned into the room.

His room appeared different than the little boy's. It was more similar to the hospital room he had envisioned. There was a hospital bed with white sheets and a light-blue blanket. A machine was beside it, wires coming out of it like a mechanical octopus. The fluorescent light was bright and made Jason squint in the contrast of the comparatively dim hallway.

Jason walked over and put his bag down on the bed. He slipped his light jacket off and hung it on the hook provided. Jason noticed three cameras mounted to the ceiling and a small half bathroom with a toilet and sink in the far corner.

"Please make yourself comfortable; Dr. Luu will be in shortly to see you."

"Thanks," Jason said, wondering if getting comfortable was going to be possible here.

He put his phone down on the side table and noticed there was no drawer.

Probably for the best, he thought as he made his way to the bathroom.

He didn't hear Dr. Luu enter his room while he was washing his hands, so Jason jumped back an inch when he turned around again.

"Shit!" Jason's heart thumped twice in his chest. "Scared the hell outta me, doc."

"Sorry about that, Jason. I didn't mean to startle you."

The doctor stood at the foot of the bed, holding a tablet against his chest.

"Shall we begin?"

* * *

Bubbles fizzed and popped against Samantha's soft skin. Gentle music was playing softly in the background as she breathed in the calming aroma of lavender and chamomile. The water was warm and soothing to her tense muscles.

She often enjoyed a nice bath after an evening yoga session, but it had been some time since she practiced. Too many distractions, she thought. Not in the right headspace. Ironically, part of doing yoga was getting you and keeping you in a positive headspace.

But we don't always do what's best for us, do we? No, she agreed with herself.

Sam sank herself deeper into the soapy water. Her dark hair was tied up with the only piece of fabric that she wore. White froth hugged against the parts of her body that would not be drowned below the surface. Her breasts floated like two desert islands upon which any pirate would gladly strangle his own mother to be stranded.

She tried to relax.

It worked, to an extent, but her thoughts kept dwelling on Jason and how the test was going. She thought he would have texted her when he got there, but he hadn't. She still hoped for a text before he went to bed. Maybe he would. She sat up, reached over and tapped her phone to check the time, then took a sip of tea. She slid back down the smooth tub until most of her body was submerged again.

Samantha wondered if Jason would be able to sleep there, in some foreign bed. She wondered if she would sleep herself. It had been so long since she slept alone. She usually didn't like it, finding it cold and lonely, but she was looking forward to this evening, hoping that without Jason and his disturbances, she would finally get a good night's rest.

She slipped further down and let her head enter the warm water. Her head floated with her ears just below the surface, the liquid muffling the apartment's sound.

One could rent a sensory deprivation chamber here in the city, Sam thought. One of those where you just float in water inside a small room. The lack of sound and light, with the feeling of floating, is meant to deprive your mind of stimuli, which does interesting and strange things to it.

People have reported having full hallucinations or communions with nature or God.

Sam wouldn't mind that here, in her bathtub. To talk to God and ask why it's so necessary for people to suffer. Samantha floated, mesmerized by the sound of water lapping against her body and the walls of the tub. She lay there until the water became still and another sound broke through. It wasn't the sound she had hoped for, though. Instead of God, all she could hear was the hum.

* * *

"So you're gonna hook me up to the Kraken are ya?"

Jason eyed the large machine that sat ominously beside his bed. Dr. Luu laughed sincerely, "Oh, no, Jason, that machine is quite old and a little outdated. It would work, but for your specific circumstances, we will use the wireless probes. Please, have a seat."

Jason sat down on the side of the bed, and Dr. Luu took a seat in the short, blue chair across from him.

"Basically, Jason, we're going to monitor your brain with our sensors while you sleep and hopefully catch any abnormalities that may be causing the disturbances. We will also monitor you physically by way of the cameras on the ceiling."

Jason looked up at the cameras and suddenly wondered if they could see him in the bathroom. Better remember to close the door next time, he thought.

"Sounds good, Doc."

"Do you normally wear pajamas to bed?"

"Actually, I usually sleep naked."

Dr. Luu raised an eyebrow.

"Well, you'll have to wear at least the shorts we asked you to bring."

"No problem, Doc."

"So, if you will kindly change, a nurse will be in shortly to attach the probes."

Jason stood up and grabbed his bag.

"Just…one more thing Jason, if you would."

Jason stopped, waiting for the doctor to continue. "Please

remain in this room now and until you are dismissed in the morning."

Jason frowned, curious.

"It's for your safety and the safety of our other patients and, of course, the staff."

"Sure, Doc, no worries."

Jason turned to go to the bathroom to change but paused and looked back at Dr. Luu.

"What if I sleepwalk out into the hall?"

"Well, that's a whole other thing entirely, Jason." With a nod, Dr. Luu turned and left, leaving Jason standing in the doorway of the bathroom, wondering what the hell the doctor meant by that.

Jason had thought the nurse would be in right away to attach the probes to his head. Instead, he was sitting shirtless in bed, looking down at his blue gym shorts. The waist fit more snugly than the last time he had worn them. He hadn't been to the gym in months, and it showed. His normally flat abdomen had piled on a layer of fat and hung lazily over his waistband. His chest sagged and looked unhappy from above. "Ok, it's friggin' gym time tomorrow. This is getting out of control."

Jason poked and squeezed at his chubby pecs and belly, but he suddenly stopped when he remembered the cameras. His eyes shot up to one of the dark, ever-seeing lenses—its dim, red light sitting sentry as it stared at him. Unblinking, always watching.

Could they hear him?

Jason pictured some lab coat on the other end of the camera feed, smiling and laughing at the fat boy spectacle. What kind of creepy bastard watches other people sleep anyway?

Jason got up from the bed and went to his bag. It opened

with a loud *ziiiiiip*. He removed a plain, white t-shirt and pulled it over his head.

Peep show's over, creeper, he thought and walked over to the window.

The large single-pane window was old. Not as old as the building, but every time the wind picked up, Jason could hear a quiet whistle as the air pushed through cracks.

He looked down at his SUV. The reliable machine that had delivered them safely all the way across the country. Over the plains and through the mountains. Who drives across the country in the middle of winter anyway? Jason mused as he eyed his vehicle with a smile. He pulled his phone from his pocket to text Sam.

"At the clinic, just waiting for them to come hook up the machine. How are you?"

Jason opened the news app and scrolled before receiving the reply: "Oh ok. Just had a bath, in bed relaxing." And a heart emoji.

Jason longed to be there too, with her, in their bed, their body heat mingling under the covers.

I gotta do this though, he thought. Hopefully, it works, hopefully…

His door opened, and a nurse walked in, pushing a cart. The cart was a chrome cornucopia of technology. Red and green lights blinked sporadically on computer panels and instruments, and black wires traveled up and down and in and out. On top sat the probes, eager to get to work.

"Hi-tech!" Jason called as he walked towards the bed.

"Good evening Mr. Steele. May I ask that you put your mask on while I set you up here? You may remove it when I'm gone."

"Whoops, sorry about that." Jason grabbed his surgical mask from the side table and slipped the straps around his ears.

"Still not completely used to that yet."

"Not a problem at all," the nurse said.

Her green eyes sparkled above her own mask as she spoke. Jason's eyes locked with hers until she broke the connection by looking down at her cart. She continued in and around the side of the bed. Jason moved slowly out of her way, unable to stop his eyes from taking in the way her red scrubs hugged all the right places of her body perfectly. Each plump cheek rose and fell as she walked, half bent over the cart she was pushing.

Jason forced his eyes away partly because it was rude to stare, partly because he knew the cameras were watching.

* * *

Samantha lay in bed, thumbing through her phone. News, weather, social media. She sighed with boredom and looked over at the empty side of the bed. Jason's side was cold and dark, and loneliness poked at her heart. She thought about how long it had been since she slept alone. When she first started dating Jason, she supposed. What was it like then? What would life be like now if she had never met Jason? She wouldn't be all the way out in Seattle, that's for sure. Away from everything and everyone she knew.

She would talk to Jason about moving back home, she thought, finally allowing herself to admit she was truly unhappy. She was sure he would, at least eventually; he wasn't happy either. COVID had thrown a wrench in the plan, but even without the global pandemic, Sam knew she would not have been happy out here.

Moving during a pandemic would probably be difficult, she thought, and likely dangerous. They could catch the virus at the gas pumps, at restaurants, at hotels. The thought of that saddened her. How we took life before for granted, she thought as she rolled over onto her other side, plugged in her phone, and set it on the table.

She clicked off the lamp and rolled onto her back, staring up at the ceiling. With a deep breath, she pulled the blanket up to her chin and allowed her eyes to close.

* * *

"How does that feel?" the nurse asked as she stepped back from affixing the last probe to Jason's face. She turned to the machine she had wheeled in earlier and began clicking buttons and toggling switches.

"Not too bad," Jason replied. "Although I feel a bit like some kids' science experiment."

Jason chuckled. His nerves were showing more than he would have liked, but the nurse didn't seem to notice or care. There were eight probes taped to his face. Eight wires sprouted from under each piece of medical tape, then hooked into a small black box fastened to his chest.

The box blinked with two small lights, and Jason found himself smiling.

"I look a bit like Vader, don't you think?"

His nerves calmed as he pictured himself strong with the force.

The nurse turned and bent over him again; her breasts

strained against her clothing as she adjusted a probe that wasn't picking up signal.

Jason could see nothing else but her chest, a few inches from his face. He tried not to look and even considered closing his eyes, but he was only a man after all. His shorts grew under the thin blanket as the perky breasts floated in front of his face, teasing him.

She's doing this on purpose! he thought. She didn't need to be right in my face with those; she could stand off to the side. What does she think? I'm just gonna grab her and pull her onto the bed, on to me? Tear her tight shirt and constricting bra off to get a good look at those puppies?

His groin grew again at the thought.

Like what? She's just gonna jump on top of me and start riding me in front of these cameras? Put on a show for the perverts?

His member stood at full attention now, ready for action, warm with blood.

What a slut!

His thoughts were interrupted when the nurse finished attaching the new probe and leaned back to look at it. Jason quickly and discreetly tucked his hardon under the waistband of his shorts to hide it. The nurse leaned back and pushed a button on the black chest monitor. She seemed satisfied as the machine beeped and the lights turned from red to green.

"There we are," she said as she tinkered with the machine on the cart. "Now, just relax and let the monitor do its thing. If you need anything, please press the button on the remote attached to your bed, and someone will be in to help. You can sleep however you normally sleep, the probes shouldn't come off, and if you need to go to the bathroom, that is fine as well. Again, we ask that you stay in your room until the test is concluded in the morning."

She waited for a moment, her glassy eyes piercing his as if searching for what lay behind them.

"Oh...ok, thank you," Jason stammered.

He suddenly felt very guilty about his thoughts. Could the machine pick up what he was thinking about? Wouldn't that be embarrassing? Imagine if people could read each other's thoughts...then we'd know just how sick everyone really is!

"Any questions?" she asked, eyes still piercing.

"No, I think I'm good here, thanks again."

The nurse bowed her head slightly and then left, closing the door behind her with a click. Jason stared after her. His eyes moved to the black box on his chest, then to the camera.

It was watching. Constantly. Judging him.

Jason looked away quickly. He grabbed his phone, texted Sam goodnight, and turned off the lights—quite tired and ready for sleep.

* * *

Samantha's eyes flew open, but no other part of her body would move. Her eyes rolled around in her unmoving head feverishly. Pure terror grasped her and held her still. She fought against the fear; she fought against the invisible hands holding her down. She tried to scream or yell for help, but all that escaped her lips was soundless air. A single, shiny tear fell from her eye and streaked her cheek with salt. It was as if all the breath inside her had been taken and not allowed back in.

She had fallen off the jungle gym again; the wind knocked completely out of her. She gasped and struggled like a drowning goldfish. Her lips puckered and pursed in a futile effort to draw breath. Her skin turned purple, and veins popped against the strain.

Find your breath, Sam, find your breath. It's a night terror; you've had this before. You're ok. You're ok.

Suddenly the invisible hands let go, receding into the night. Her lungs again accepted air as she sucked it in greedily. She sat up and clutched her chest, her breathing heavy and labored. She continued to sit until she calmed down once again. Her heart rate eventually slowed and normalized. Saliva came back to moisten her dry mouth. The few beads of sweat on her forehead dried in the night air. Her breathing relaxed and became natural again, but instead of silence in the gaps between inhale and exhale, she heard only the hum. Samantha sat still for a moment, listening. She hated that sound. She hated hearing it, and she hated what it was doing to Jason.

"Fuck you, hum," she said quietly as she lay back and turned on her Bluetooth speaker.

CHAPTER 21

"I THINK HE LIKES YOU."

"Of course he does," the nurse replied. "Who?"

"The guy in 2D. Let's just say he was at full attention when you were strapping him in."

"Don't be vile, Jerry."

Jerry spun around in his chair and began clicking away on his keyboard. In front of him were eight large monitors showing video feeds of rooms inside the sleep clinic.

"I'm not even kidding Amanda; this guy likes you!" Jerry hooted with the maturity of a schoolyard bully. "Here, let me back up the recording so you can see for yourself."

He clicked a button and spun a dial, and the bottom left monitor's video began moving backward.

"Whatever, I don't care," Amanda said as she walked over to her station. Her desk was a copy of Jerry's. Eight monitors lit up her face as she sat down. She looked at each screen, carefully studying their feeds to make sure everything, and everyone, was in order. Satisfied, she began working on her end-of-shift notes. Nothing out of the ordinary tonight, she thought, just the usual tired-looking people desperately searching for help.

The men were the easiest to handle. Sure, sometimes they leered uncomfortably long and talked to her like she was a dumb blonde, but she would just give them a cute look and flavor her words with sugar, and they would be easily mallea-ble. Malleable. That's a word she knew because she was de-cidedly not a dumb blonde. She was working on her masters, and soon she would have her Ph.D.

Beauty and brains, a lethal combo, as Jerry would say. But the men were the easiest—even the old, lecherous ones. None had been so bold as to fully grab her, but sometimes she would get a waft of gold bond and mothballs as a frail, boney hand 'accidentally' brushed her breasts on its way to adjust a shirt or glasses.

The first time it happened, Amanda had recoiled in sur-prise and disgust, but the feeble old man looking up at her from the bed had a playful smile and glint in his eyes that made her relax. It wasn't like one of the frat boys at her college; this was an old man. Death wasn't far off, and he just wanted to feel the warm skin and firm fat of a young woman's chest. Hard to blame him, really.

The women were more difficult. Usually, they were ok, more self-absorbed in whatever was troubling their sleep, but Amanda noticed the looks. The look from these tired, usually middle-aged housewives was a mix between jealousy and hate. Maybe not hate. Amanda didn't feel hate from these women as much as resentment. As if it was beautiful, young, thin, pretty Amanda's fault that their husbands would rather jerk off on the internet than fuck their aging wives.

It wasn't conceit; people had been telling her that she was beautiful her whole life. As a child, she was told she was "going to be a heartbreaker," and as a teen, they said to her father, "I bet you have to beat the boys off with a stick."

Now, as a young adult, the boys she wanted to talk to

her were too shy, and the boys who did only seemed to want one thing.

Still, Amanda didn't blame these ladies for the way they looked her up and down when she entered the room with the sleep device—she pitied them and swore she would never end up that way.

The children who came to the clinic were her favorites, but they were often the most difficult for her emotionally. Amanda had little sympathy for the adults. She cared; she really did want them to feel better, but she could turn off any emotion or attachment to the outcome. After a few years in this field, she had realized that most of the issues, the things causing sleep problems with people, seemed to be of their own making. The specter of their own guilt and pain and re-gret disturbing their sleep like a menacing ghost that could be simply banished if they would just let go of those feelings. Often, all the patients needed were some tests and a good talk or two with Dr. Luu—more psychologist than somnol-ogist. They learned stress management and relaxation tech-niques. They discovered the correlation between the health of the body and the health of the mind. It was amazing what a little exercise and a proper diet could do to improve the quality of your sleep.

Sometimes this worked for the children as well. They might just need some exercise and to augment their diet. Sometimes they could be taught relaxation techniques as well and how to deal with negative self-talk.

But if the ghosts that haunted them weren't of their own making, then what could be done?

Amanda loved walking in and finding a child in the room that she could make smile and laugh. A child with an open heart, fully accepting of love, laughter, and joy. But when she opened the door and walked into a room occupied by a truly sad and depressed child, a child that would not laugh and would force themself to crack the faintest of smiles at a joke, it almost made her want to quit. To get into a field that won't put that sadness on her. Selfish, Amanda thought, and impossible.

She could never drag herself away. She loved the success stories too much. She loved seeing that same depressed child a month later, looking well rested and alive. That is why she did this work: to help people. And to crack those incredibly fascinating and strange cases.

Cases like the boy in 2B.

Amanda's eyes floated from the screen where she had just finished her nightly report to the monitor showing the boy in 2B. There he lay with the covers pulled tight up to his chest. His blue and white pinstriped pajamas covered his shoulders. His shaggy brown hair stood out like winter wheat against the white pillowcase. He lay completely still, quietly and unblinkingly staring at the camera lens and right back into Amanda's eyes.

CHAPTER 22

"**G**OOD MORNING MR. STEELE!" SAID A BRIGHT voice from a crack in the door after a quick knock. "Are you decent?"

"I'm sure you know I'm decent; you've been watching me all night."

Jerry opened the door and gave a little wave. He walked over to the bed and began removing the probes from Jason's head.

"Well, now, I wasn't watching you all night Mr. Steele…"

"Jason."

"Oh, ok, Jason. We always have one person on in case of emergency. Mostly I watched YouTube videos and napped." Jerry winked.

Below his eyes, Jerry's mask was black with white sheep jumping over little brown fences.

"The name's Jerry."

His voice was almost shrill; that pitch one hits when they are forcing cheerfulness. It put Jason off. Or maybe Jason was just disappointed that Jerry was Jerry instead of the nurse from the night before. Instead of Jerry's fake enthusiasm and stupid mask, Jason would have much preferred to have her perfect, perky breasts in his face. Jason's groin began to swell again at the thought of her. Realizing this, he caught the thought and stopped it cold.

They weren't that great, Jesus man, get it together.

Jason shook his head slightly.

"So you didn't see if I was talkin' or moving around last night?" he asked.

"Huh-uh, no sir. I have an alarm set to check on the monitors every hour." His eyes fell away from Jason's. "Every time I looked, you were just lying there."

Jerry set a probe down on the machine and reached for another.

"So you just had quick little naps then."

Jason studied Jerry for any signs that he might be hiding something that he saw. Like when you go to get x-rays and ask the technician if everything looks ok and they reply that they aren't allowed to say. Was that pity in their eyes? Did they see something? Is it the big C?

After removing the last probe and the black box from Jason's chest, Jerry looked back at Jason.

"Yes sir, just quick little catnaps."

Jason nodded, convinced that Jerry had spent most of the night not watching the monitors closely at all. Something in Jerry's eyes told Jason that Jerry's 'quick little catnaps' were probably more like he slept the whole damn night through, and that was why he was so fresh and annoying.

Jerry piled all the wires onto the machine with the black Vader box, wheeled it about a foot from the bed, and turned to Jason.

"Dr. Luu will let you know the results at the follow-up appointment you set for Wednesday at four o'clock. It takes a bit of time to review the data. Do you have any questions for me, Mr. sorry, Jason?" Jason spun his legs over the side of the bed and stretched.

"Nope, I'm good. Thanks, Jerry."

With that, Jerry turned and wheeled the machine out the door, leaving it open. Jason looked over at the side table. Everything that was supposed to be there was there. Nothing out of place or moved around. Disappointment colored Jason's face. He was hoping he had moved things around. He hoped that he talked and elbowed and swore. He hoped that he got up and did a damn sleepwalking jig. Only so the doctor could see what the hell was going on in his brain when it happened. Oh well, he thought, sleeping Jerry may have missed something after all. Just going to have to wait and see.

Jason stood up, bent over for another stretch, and then headed into the bathroom to relieve himself. As he passed the mirror, he stopped.

"Man, you're looking old," he said to his reflection. The hair at his temples had started greying recently, and now that it had grown out, the grey was very noticeable. The bags under his eyes were like fluid-filled sacks tugging at his lower eyelids. His beard was getting grey at the sides too, and needed a trim.

Jason stared into his reflection's eyes. They were deep, dark blue, like the color of an angry ocean.

Hair turns grey and skin becomes loose and lined, but the eyes remain unchanged. Jason stared a moment longer into the ocean, attempting to see below the rough surface, into his own soul.

His concentration was broken by voices from the hallway. The person from the room across the hall was leaving. Jerry's voice sounded shrill.

Jason relieved himself, washed his hands, and then brushed his teeth. He spat and rinsed, then looked briefly into the reflection's dark eyes, daring them to reveal what lay below the surface.

With a deep breath of resignation, Jason grabbed his toiletries and left the bathroom, turning off the light as he passed.

He dressed quickly, suddenly hungry and missing Samantha, and headed out the door.

Three of the doors were open in the hallway.

All except 2B. The room where he had seen the boy the night before. That strange little boy dressed like a grown man. He had looked like a grown man, really—a grown man in a child's body. Jason shivered as he passed the closed door, anxious to get home.

* * *

Samantha poured a glass of orange juice and took a long drink. The sweet wetness coated her mouth and cooled her throat as it fell to her stomach. She gasped a little from holding her breath, took in another deep lungful, and finished the glass. The sugar and vitamins seemed to invigorate her instantly as she stood in the kitchen.

Jason had just texted; he would be home soon.

Thank God, she thought. Being alone was difficult enough, but tack on a pandemic and the pregnancy and this damn apartment with the constant hum.

Jason hadn't mentioned anything; he had just texted, "Be home soon."

Sam moved to the window and looked out at the harbor. The sun's reflection on the water looked like thousands of diamonds shining brilliantly upon a blue blanket. People were milling about below, out for their Sunday morning walks.

Some shops were open now, as long as they sold food, but their capacities had been greatly reduced, creating long lines outside. On a day like today, though, standing outside was a gift. The notorious wet and dreary Seattle spring weather had lived up to its reputation this year, so a gorgeous break like today felt amazing.

It felt like hope.

Hope that a vaccine would come quickly. Hope that things would get back to normal. Hope that Dr. Luu could do something for Jason, and even if he could not, a sliver of hope that she could convince Jason to move home.

Home and away.

Away from the rain and clouds. Away from the isolation. Away from the visions of the hiker that had tainted her memories of the mountains. She didn't care if she ever saw mountains again.

We were happier at home, she thought. It wasn't perfect, but at least we had family and friends. We had support.

If I told him how sad I am, how lonely, surely he—the locking mechanism inside the door came to life, and its insides moved with metallic clicks.

Samantha gathered her white robe and her senses and went to the door, wondering how long she had been standing at the window.

"Hey, cutie!" Jason smiled as he entered the apartment. Samantha smiled back easily but impatiently waited for him to touch her. Jason put down his duffle, kicked off his boots, and grabbed Samantha tightly around the waist. She let out a quick squeal as Jason lifted her into the air.

She wrapped her arms around his neck and kissed him deeply and with intent.

"Well?" Samantha was out of breath as he put her down. "How was it?"

"Weird. Really weird. Just an odd place filled with odd people. The only normal person there was Dr. Luu, and I only saw him for a minute."

"Oh?" Samantha turned and walked into the kitchen to make breakfast.

"Yeah, it's all good. They just hooked up a machine to my head, turned the cameras on, and left me alone."

Jason pulled out a stool and sat down on it.

"I was pretty beat by then, so I basically went right to sleep. I asked the guy in the morning, the nurse I guess, if he saw anything, and he said no. I'll bet he was asleep at the wheel all night. He seemed well rested anyway."

Yellow scrambled eggs seared loudly against the hot pan. Samantha threw the empty egg carton out into the blue bin under the sink, then rinsed her hands. She popped a few pieces of bread into the toaster and turned to face Jason.

He smiled.

He looked good, she thought. Like a night away from this damn apartment was all he needed to get back to the Jason she knew before.

"Your follow-up is Wednesday?"

"Yeah, I wish it wouldn't take so long, but I guess it takes time to go over the data and the video recording and all that." Jason paused for a moment. "And there were at least three other people there, on my floor. Four rooms. And there are another four rooms on the third floor, I think."

Jason licked his lips.

"God, that smells good. Thanks for taking care of me, babe."

Jason's voice turned sentimental.

"I don't know what I'd do without you."

Sam stirred the eggs and turned off the burner.

The bread had become toast, so Sam grabbed each piece nimbly and ran butter across their faces.

In a flash of movement, the food was on the plates. She she sat down beside Jason and poured them each a glass of orange juice.

"I don't know what you'd do without me either," Sam teased.

"Well, I wouldn't eat as well, that's for sure," Jason said with forced machismo.

He picked up a warm piece of toast and popped it into his mouth.

* * *

"Do you miss home?" Samantha asked as they lay in bed. The day had been well spent. The couple relaxed in the morning and then made love in the shower. They had gone for a long walk, since the clear morning had turned into a beautiful and warm afternoon. They shared an order of fish and chips from a takeout restaurant on the seawall and followed it up with a cup of gelato. When they returned home, they had made love again, but on the couch this time, the tall, uncovered living room windows allowing the late-day sun to warm their naked bodies.

After dinner, they had watched a couple of funny movies while cuddling on the couch, occasionally snacking on chips from a bowl on the coffee table.

A near perfect day, Sam thought. But even so, her heart yearned for home, and she wanted to know if Jason's did too.

"Yeah." Jason paused. "But it's pretty sweet out here, don't you think?" Sam frowned, but Jason was on his back, staring at the ceiling.

"I mean, this COVID thing kinda fucked everything up, and I guess the thing on the mountain wasn't great. And I haven't been sleeping very well at all…" Jason trailed off.

Samantha waited; was he now realizing this place wasn't "pretty sweet" at all? Surely he had to see how bad things had been.

"But I dunno. There are a lot of cool things out here, and without the pandemic, I think we'd be having a great time right now." Jason's words were sincere and hopeful. He looked over at Samantha, who hadn't responded at all.

"But this COVID thing did mess everything up, Jason."

Her words were sharp and stated matter-of-factly. "It's kept us trapped in this tiny apartment, isolated and alone. I can't find work right now; you don't seem all that interested in what you do."

"Hey now," Jason tried to interject, but Samantha would not relent. She sat up and stared into his eyes.

"Well? You don't. You're like a damn zombie in there staring at the screen. Is this really what you want for yourself? For us?" Her voice became shrill, and the pace of her words quickened.

"I'm scared, Jason! Really scared! Of this place, of what it's doing to you! How you are, what you've become. Shining your goddamn shotgun in your sleep? What the hell is that!?"

Samantha's voice cracked slightly as she finished her unplanned rant. Tears burst from her eyes and rolled down her cheeks and onto the bedding. She covered her face with trembling hands and sobbed uncontrollably.

Jason grimaced.

He sat up, put his hand on her back, and rubbed soothingly.

"I'm sorry, babe," he said softly.

Her sobs slowed a little at his touch. "I'm sorry, but I don't know what to do about it. Are we just supposed to pack up and leave?"

He paused for effect.

"What about my job? What about our lease? Where would we even go? Back to Scranton?" His voice became indignant. "So what? Mommy and Daddy can take care of you?"

Jason's nostrils flared, and the words tasted sour and hot as they left his tongue. Samantha's sobs stopped, and she removed her hands from her puffy, wet face. She stared at Jason the way only someone who has been deeply hurt by a person they love can stare. Jason's hard expression softened at the sight of the pain in Sam's dark eyes. He looked away with a touch of shame.

Samantha got out of bed and walked to the bathroom, not bothering to turn on the light. She ran cool water and splashed it over her face. She reached for a towel and dried herself off. Jason heard her blow her nose and then saw her reemerge from the dark bathroom. She got back into bed, turned her lamp off with a click, and pulled the covers up to her chin, facing away from Jason. He sat quietly a little longer, staring at the wall, going over what had just happened in his head. With a deep sigh, he lay down, pulled the covers up, and turned his lamp off as well.

CHAPTER 23

J ASON'S BODY TWITCHED AS HE FLOATED THROUGH the thick and heavy veil between the sleep realm and reality. Disturbing, uncomfortable images faded away beneath him as consciousness stirred and regained control. His brain began the process of firing up to allow his senses to transmit information to it once more.

Jason could hear the wind whipping around the building, coming and going in prolonged bursts; the distant, busy traffic sounds of rubber on concrete and muffled engine roars.

His mouth was dry and bitter, which made him lick his parched lips and swallow in an attempt to summon lubricant.

Early morning light threatened entry on the other side of his closed eyelids. He fought the urge to open them, clinging to the last dregs of sleep.

He filled his lungs through his nose, recognizing the sweet smell of Samantha's bodywash that he had helped apply to her back the day before. Lavender and honeysuckle; sweet and delicate, just like her.

There was something else, though, another smell. Something dull and metallic. The images that had receded back under the dream veil flashed again in his mind's eye, quickly and clearly.

Jason instinctively reached out to touch Samantha to make sure she was there. His panic calmed slightly as his hand found purchase. His eyes flew open, and the images receded back down into their watery void.

He lay watching Sam, his hand now resting gently on her stomach. The cotton of her shirt was soft against his palm. She was so still—her face like marble, calm and serene. Jason slowly moved his hand down across Sam's pelvis to grab the meat of her thigh.

His hand found something wet and thick.

Jason rubbed the pad of his thumb against his forefinger. Viscose liquid, neither warm nor cold. Jason's banished images crashed back into his mind with a flash of lightning and pain.

His heart sank and fluttered in his chest, skipping beats as it pounded against his ribcage. Beads of cold sweat squeezed through his pores and onto his skin. The complete racks of fear took control. Jason had been elbow deep in enough deer carcasses to know the unique viscosity of blood.

And now it was on his hands again.

But there were no deer, no wild game, not even the hiker. There was only Sam.

Oh my God! His mind raced. His body solid and stuck; it would not move. He could only stare at Sam.

Was she breathing?

He couldn't tell.

Was her damn chest moving!? Shit! I don't know! There's no way. No fucking way!

It's just a dream, a bad dream about the hiker again, looking up at me with hollow, dead eyes.

Jason forced his hand to move. He had to know. He pulled his trembling hand up and out from under the blanket and stared at it in horror. He could do nothing but stare. Slack-jawed and numb, he stared at his bloody palm, not wanting to believe, but the evidence was right there, right in front of his face, smelling dull and metallic.

He had killed her.

He had killed her in his goddamn sleep.

The images weren't dreams; they were memories. Memories of killing his fucking girlfriend and—wait. She stirred?

She stirred!

Jason's thoughts came to a complete and utter stop as his gaze moved from his bloody hand to Samantha. She was looking at his hand now too.

He blinked.

He wanted to talk, to say anything, but he couldn't. Samantha looked at Jason and then back at his hand with disgusted puzzlement.

"Jay?" she asked, then fainted.

"Sam?" Jason said flatly.

His thoughts were racing. Finally his body sprang into action.

"Babe!?"

Jason reached down, touched her face, and moved it back and forth. His bloody, shaking hand moved from her chin bone to her neck. He pressed two fingers against the warm flesh above the carotid artery. Samantha's life force bumped against his fingers in slow, powerful waves. Jason sighed with heavy relief.

"Oh, thank God." He jumped to his knees beside her and threw the blankets back in one quick flail of movement.

"Jesus," he said as he scanned her body. He had expected to see dark-red gashes surrounded by bright crimson liquid soaking the fabric of her shirt. Images of the hiker's punctured body raced across his thoughts.

Blood had stained Samantha's shirt, but only at the bottom. Below that, her shorts, the cute ones with pictures of stars and half-moons she slept in, were wet and thick with blood.

Jason stared at Sam's pelvis with confusion. It was blood, that was clear. But it wasn't the fresh, bright blood of a newly opened wound. No, this was something different, something from inside, from—"The baby!" Jason said with sudden realization and horror.

"Oh, no, oh no."

Sorrow and pain smacked him dumb as he fully realized the consequences of the bloody shorts.

"Fuck," he said as he moved to grab his phone from the nightstand. He picked it up and began to punch in his passcode, smearing the screen with blood.

"Jay?" A soft whimper of a voice.

Jason turned around. Samantha was staring at him with the saddest eyes he'd ever seen. Her hands had instinctually went to her stomach, holding it, protecting it.

"You're ok, babe. You're ok."

Jason rolled back and knelt beside her. He touched her face.

"I'm calling 911 right now; you're ok."

"No."

"What?"

"No, no ambulance, Jason."

"But we have to go to the hospital!" Jason roared out in anger marked with fear.

"We will. You can drive me. Just let me get cleaned up."

Samantha's words came calm and authoritatively. The contrast was stark against Jason's frantic, pleading tone.

Samantha sat up and looked down at herself. Jason watched her as her face remained calm. Calm but sad and without any fear. Jason relaxed some as he realized she wasn't in any immediate danger. She was conscious and coherent. She wasn't bleeding to death. He hadn't stabbed her sixteen times and left her for dead in the woods.

"Ok," he said flatly.

Samantha got up and headed to the laundry room, leaving Jason staring after her dumbly. She removed her soiled shirt and shorts and deposited them into the washer. She threw a detergent pod in with them and turned the machine on, doubting the clothes would come out clean. She emerged from the laundry room naked and made her way to the bathroom, where she found her tampons, took one out, inserted it, and cranked on the shower.

She got in quickly and shivered against the cool water as she waited for it to warm. Jason got up from the bed and stripped it of its sheet. The blood had soaked through to the mattress cover, so he removed that as well. He took the fitted sheet and mattress cover to the washing machine, opened it up, stopping the cycle, and added the sheets. He tossed in another pod for good measure and restarted the machine.

As he passed the bathroom, he looked inside. Samantha was sitting cross-legged under the cone of water. He paused a moment when he heard soft, slow sobs coming from the shower.

Jason thought to ask her if she was ok but decided against it. The best thing he could do right now, he thought, was to get ready to take her in.

* * *

The visit to the hospital was long and stressful. There were questionnaires and surveys to complete and sign. COVID posters hung on the walls with colorful depictions of the virus, a red "X" drawn to show the virus wasn't welcome here. There were warnings posted everywhere, along with several security guards. Even though Samantha and Jason had arrived at the emergency department early in the day, there were already many people in the waiting room.

Jason helped Sam find a place to sit and then went to the desk to register. The nurse was visibly stressed and anxious. It was clear to Jason that the staff was stretched thin and over-worked during the pandemic. After registering, the tired nurse asked Jason to take a seat and wait to be called.

The couple sat waiting for hours as sick and desperate people came and went, wearing masks and sanitizing their hands constantly. Some people wore expensive respirator masks and goggles, their hands wrapped in gloves. The tension in their muscles was visible. The fear in their eyes was palpable.

It was scary to even look at, like witnessing a nuclear ho-locaust or chemical warfare.

Dressed in two layers of scrubs, wearing gloves, N95 masks, and face shields, nurses would periodically call a few names before disappearing again behind the big, automatic doors.

Finally, the nurse called Samantha's name, and they too were invited back behind the doors.

The room behind the doors was large and filled with beds. Around each bed and its accompanying small plastic chair hung a long, blue curtain. The nurse led them to their destination and drew the curtain around them as they waited for the doctor. Jason sat on the small plastic chair, and Samantha hopped up on the hospital bed, the fresh paper crinkling and crunching beneath her as she moved.

They could hear everything that was going on in the emergency room: someone had been stabbed in the leg, someone's husband beat them up, a little boy had broken his arm falling out of the top bunk. Jason thought he heard hushed talk from a woman complaining to a doctor that it burned when she peed. Jason cringed and looked up at Samantha. She was lying back with her hands clasped and resting on her belly, staring up at the ceiling. She felt Jason staring and looked over at him and smiled. Just a soft, "I'm ok, babe" kind of smile.

His lips pinched together, and he nodded and looked away.

Where is the damn doctor? he thought impatiently, tapping his foot to some unheard frantic beat.

He tried at a fingernail, but there weren't any long enough to bite. He gnawed absently at a finger and frowned at the sharp, bitter taste of alcohol against his tongue. He scraped the top of his tongue against his teeth and wondered how three months of tasting rubbing alcohol hadn't deterred him from chewing the shit out of his nails.

As Jason pondered this, a gloved hand appeared through a crack in the curtain and pushed it aside.

Finally, Jason thought and sat up straight in his small, plastic chair. The doctor inspected Samantha and asked her several questions. He said with the amount of blood she described, it was likely a miscarriage but could have also been a period. The only way to know for sure was to order blood tests and an ultrasound. He would have the results sent to Dr. Greene's office, where Samantha had been before, and they would contact her with the news. The doctor said the nurse would be in shortly to give them the requisition forms, wished them well, and then exited though the curtain.

Samantha and Jason looked at each other silently. Neither of them could think of anything to say. Both knew nothing needed to be said.

Jason stood up and went to Samantha. He kissed her forehead and brushed her dark hair soothingly as they waited. A nurse soon pulled back the curtain. Samantha sat up and spun her legs so they fell over the side of the bed.

The nurse handed some forms to Samantha, said a curt "take care," and left, leaving the curtain wide open in an invitation for the couple to leave. Jason and Samantha looked at each other again; the shared sadness weighing heavily in their eyes.

Jason moved to stand in-between Samantha's legs and hugged her hard and close. She allowed a few tears to escape her damp eyes as they embraced. Then, once she felt like she could go on, they let go and left the hospital.

* * *

Back home in the early afternoon, Samantha and Jason could finally sit down and try to relax. Jason's work had allowed him to take the day off without too much explanation, and the bloodwork and ultrasound were completed quickly at a clinic only a block away from the hospital. Now it was just time to wait. Wait and try to relax.

Samantha changed out of her street clothes into grey

track pants and a long-sleeved shirt. Jason sat down on the couch, grabbed the tv remote, and put his crossed legs up on the coffee table all in one slick, fluid motion.

Samantha appeared from the bedroom. She sat down beside Jason and kissed him on the cheek. She lay down with her head on a pillow and her feet up on Jason's lap. He watched her relax into the couch, her breath slowing and becoming more even. Her body twitched slightly, and soon after that, she was out: successfully escaping this hard reality into a peaceful slumber. With a gentle squeeze of her calf, Jason looked away and turned on the television.

CHAPTER 24

Just as Samantha and Jason were getting home from the hospital, Jerry was starting his Monday shift across the city. Mondays were for reviewing recordings for Dr. Luu, and although the shift change messed with Jerry's sleep schedule, he knew he had to put in the hours.

Jerry also knew Amanda would be there, which didn't hurt. He looked over at her, taking in her curves; the roundness of her bottom against the chair.

How many times had he asked her out? Jerry thought. Three? Or four?

He got shot down every time. Not in a mean way. Amanda was too nice to be a bitch, making it that much harder not to want her.

Sexy and smart. What a combo! But so far, no luck. Maybe fifth time's a charm?

She looked up from her desk as if feeling Jerry's eyes fixed on her. He looked away quickly as she turned.

"Good weekend?" Amanda asked sweetly.

"Mmhmm, yeah," Jerry replied, trying to look busy with some papers.

"Overnight on Saturday was pretty uneventful. Slept most of the night, to be honest."

He looked over at Amanda, his eyes squinted from a hidden, toothy smile. On his mask another smile was printed on the fabric, like that of a clown. Bright red lips sneered wickedly, framing cartoonishly large and perfectly white square teeth.

It was hideous.

It was Jerry's Monday mask.

He could wear it because there were no patients to see that day, only Amanda. And sometimes Dr. Luu. "Dr. Luu is going to catch you sleeping one of these days, you know. Then what?"

"Then I won't be able to spend my Mondays with you," Jerry replied.

His words were thick with fake affection, the kind that is made to sound like a joke, but underneath it lay the truth.

"Exactly," she said smoothly, turning back to her work, "Then I'll have to put up with some other weirdo in a hideous mask."

They giggled lightly, but the comment stung Jerry slightly—he thought his mask was funny.

Jerry cleared his throat and tried to focus on the paperwork in front of him.

Amanda didn't realize that Jerry had failed to mention what he did on Sunday, or perhaps she didn't care. Jerry was grateful, but if she did push the subject, he would simply say "not much," skirting the topic.

On Sunday, after he kicked everyone out of the clinic and finished his reports, Jerry had jumped in his beat-up chevy and drove home. On the radio, Jerry had listened to the voice talk about a hearing coming up for that guy who stabbed the shit out of his wife up the mountains not too long ago.

Jerry thought the guy must have hated his wife an awful

lot to take her all the way up Mount Rainier and kill her like that.

Probably wasn't giving up the cooze anymore, Jerry had thought and clicked off the radio.

He kept his little apartment clean—as clean as one could make an old, rundown space. The building was likely eighty years old, and time had taken some things that could not be reclaimed with all the Javex in the world.

Jerry had gone inside, now feeling the familiar tired tingles behind his eyelids, asking him for sleep. He pulled his backpack off, then his jacket. He kicked off his boots and walked across the tiny kitchen toward his bed. His bachelor pad was truly a bachelor pad—with only two rooms—the bathroom and the everything-else room.

He pulled off his scrubs and sat on his bed wearing only his tighty-whities. He reached over the side, grabbed his laptop, and leaned back into the pillows. He pulled up one of Amanda's social media profiles and started poking around, clicking on pictures and reading updates.

Creeping is what it's called, Jerry thought.

Creeping through her pictures, he saw Amanda at school with some friends. Another post showed Amanda at a party, a little blurry-eyed and smiling her gorgeous smile. She was wearing a little black dress so tight that her perfect breasts seemed to be on the verge of popping out.

Jerry kept going, clicking further until he saw what he wanted—pictures from the trip she had taken to California with her girlfriends.

Dozens of photos of that gorgeous smile, perfect face, and scantily clad body. Her bikinis barely covered up her perfect, round breasts. Her butt cheeks spilled out of her skimpy bottoms.

And in one picture, Jerry's favorite, her pink bikini bottoms hugged everything just right—displaying a perfect camel toe.

Jerry grabbed the hand lotion and a few tissues from the nightstand and furiously masturbated before he gave in to his eyelids' demands and went to sleep.

After waking from his midday sleep, Jerry played video games, ate whatever he could heat in the microwave, and had himself another round of grinding the pepper just before bed.

What else was he going to do during a pandemic anyway? Still—he wasn't proud of his unproductive day and was not about to discuss it with Amanda.

"Who do you got?" Jerry asked, only half interested. It was a little game they played on Mondays. "Umm…"

Amanda's brow furrowed as she looked at the shining monitors in front of her.

"I got the old guy that smelled like sausage and sauerkraut, and the lady with Tourette's who kept calling me a slut cunt when I hooked her up to the machine."

Jerry laughed like an eighth grader who had just heard a fart joke, interrupting his coworker. Amanda looked over at Jerry quickly and glared.

"It's a serious condition, Jerry," she said matter-of-factly.

"I know…" Jerry snorted, "But you gotta admit, that shit's a little funny!" His ridiculous clown smile mask added to the insult, but Amanda couldn't help but smile. Jerry looked ridiculous. And it was true that a pleasant, modest-looking middle-aged woman suddenly yelling out "slut!" and "cunt!" in a halted, jerky voice was funny.

Even the poor lady herself had giggled a little after apologizing to the young nurse.

"Aaaand, oh."

Amanda paused, staring at the monitor for room 2B. "That little boy." She shivered.

"Nice," Jerry replied.

"I got the fat chick, the mobster, and that guy that couldn't stop staring at you."

"That's not nice, Jerry."

"What? He was obviously undressing you with his eyes. Here, I'll show you." Jerry started clicking away with his mouse.

"I meant calling that girl fat. She could have a glandular problem or something; you don't know." Jerry scoffed and continued clicking.

"Here, check this out."

Amanda wheeled over on her office chair, not too close, but close enough for Jerry to take her sweet scent into his lungs. He couldn't help but take a quick peek at Amanda's breasts as they settled into their spot beside him.

Another click started the recording.

It showed the man in 2D standing in shorts and a t-shirt by the window of his room. He was browsing or texting on his phone. Suddenly his door opened, and Amanda walked through wheeling in the monitoring device.

The two technicians watched the monitor closely. Jerry's breathing slowly started to get heavier, almost a pant, distracting Amanda. She tried to block it out. The recording's sound was playing through Jerry's headphones, so she couldn't hear it, but she was only interested in the video anyway. Amanda wasn't all that interested, but she knew that Jerry would be insufferable if she didn't play along.

She watched as Jason crossed the room without taking his eyes off her.

This was normal.

Men stared at her all the time, women too.

The man lay down, and the recording of herself began attaching the probes to his head; whoops, the last one wasn't on correctly, so she adjusted it.

"There!" Jerry said as he paused the video.

"What?" Amanda asked as she searched the paused video.

Jerry zoomed the camera in, then a little more.

"Oh jeez, Jerry!" Amanda's cheeks flushed. Jerry laughed, his clown teeth a sick blue color against the light of the screen.

"Mr. Steele is hard for you! Get it!? Hard!"

Jerry went off in a fit of immature laughter, actual tears forming in his eyes. The ridiculous smile on his mask matched his pitch perfectly. Amanda let out a loud groan and pushed herself away from Jerry's desk.

"'Cause steel is hard! You don't get it, do you?" Jerry continued as she fled, not consciously realizing he often had a way of taking things a little too far.

"I get it, Jerry; it's just not funny."

Amanda took a deep breath and turned to focus on her work. She brought up the first video, the little boy, and started the recording.

May as well get this one out of the way, she thought. Jerry was still snickering as he restarted his video. "Well, I'd say it's a nice compliment anyway," he finished. Amanda did not reply, but a small part of her agreed.

Jerry and Amanda's task on Mondays was fairly easy but time-consuming, depending on the subject of the recordings. They would essentially watch the video, doubling or tripling the speed until they saw something noteworthy from the slumbering subject, and then make a note of the incident.

When a subject moved in some way—rolled over, sat up, or even got up for a sleepwalk—the action and duration were noted. Or a spike would appear on the audio recording below the video, and the technician would document something like: 12:31 a.m.—Subject audible for five seconds. They did this so that the video could be compared to the brain scan data. The idea was to compare the physical and audible disturbances with the readings from the scan. As a result, the doctor could formulate certain hypotheses and diagnoses.

"Oh, looks like Mr. Hard As Steel went for a little stroll Saturday night," Jerry said as he backed the video up to locate the beginning of the disturbance. Amanda hit pause on her recording, stood up, and walked over to Jerry's desk for a stretch.

Sleepwalkers weren't a rare occurrence, but they were rare enough that it was still interesting to watch. Sleepwalkers would typically get up, walk around, maybe stand around for a bit, and then go back to bed, blissfully unaware of their strange actions.

1:34 a.m.—Subject sits up in bed.

Jerry made a note and then started the video again.

"Maybe he's just going to the bathroom," Amanda said as she leaned in closer to the screen. Maybe he would leave the door open, and she'd get a better view of Mr. Steele, she thought. He was handsome, after all. Jerry caught the look in Amanda's eye and said in an annoyed tone, "Nah, I stopped the video when he was just sitting on the edge of the bed. Oh, there he goes."

1:37 a.m.—Subject stands and walks slowly to the middle of the room.

Amanda frowned as she watched. A few minutes passed, and her attention waned. She thought about going back to the recording of the child who had rolled over a few times but had done nothing else of note so far.

She moved to leave but then froze, eyes glued to Jerry's screen. Mr. Steele was on the move again, his head slightly cocked as if trying to hear better.

1:40 a.m.—Subject moves to the wall opposite the bed.

A step, and then another, and then a few more until the sleepwalking man stopped, staring sightlessly at the wall. He reached out with both hands and ran his palms across the smooth paint.

Then something neither Amanda nor Jerry had ever seen before happened: The man pressed his ear up to the wall.

1:41 a.m.—Subject… listens to the wall?

Jerry looked up at Amanda. She looked down at him and then back at the screen.

"Well, that's new."

They continued watching for five minutes until the man moved again.

1:46 a.m.—Subject returned to bed.

On the recording, Jason could be seen climbing back under the covers. He pulled them up to his chest and appeared to go back to 'sleep.'

"So weird," Jerry scoffed. "I wonder what this guy's brain scan looks like. I bet it's a mess."

Amanda straightened up, still staring at the screen, watching Mr. Steele lying in the bed.

"Yeah," she said absentmindedly. "Let me know if he does it again, would you?"

Amanda turned and left the room rather than directly returning to her station. Jerry watched her leave, only turning back to his work once she had disappeared into the hall.

Amanda turned on the bathroom light and closed the door behind her. She locked it, pulled down her pants, and sat down on the cold toilet seat. As she passed water, she pictured Mr. Steele with his body and side of his face pressed up against the wall.

She shivered, wiped, and flushed. She pulled up her pants and washed her hands, lathering the soap between her palms.

Amanda had seen some weird stuff before. She had seen a little girl have a full-blown tea party with three invisible guests. She had seen a lady fight off a figment of her imagination that was apparently trying to hurt her. She had even seen people play with themselves or even commit sex acts with furniture in the room.

But there was something about Mr. Steele listening to the wall that chilled her to her core. Something about how his vacant eyes stared blankly at the ceiling as he stood there.

She shivered again. Most people's eyes were closed when they sleepwalked.

She finished rinsing her hands, turned off the tap, and gave herself a reassuring nod in the mirror. The whites of her green eyes were sporadically laced with thin red lines. She thought she looked older than she was when all that showed were her eyes and forehead—her youth hidden beneath the light-blue surgical mask. The mask pressed against her open mouth as she took in a deep breath and went back to work.

"Everything working properly?"

Amanda rolled her eyes. Jerry had a way of getting on her nerves. He wasn't terrible-looking, she thought. If he would cut the BS jokes all the time, some girl might even want to date him. "Everything's fine, Jerry."

She walked over to her chair and sat down. "Anything else from 2D?" she asked hesitantly, attempting not to sound too interested. It worked. "No," Jerry replied flatly. "Not yet anyway."

Amanda grabbed her mouse and clicked play on her recording. The strange little boy was still, curled up in a ball. She sped up the feed. She watched the shape under the covers for a while until he suddenly sat up. The mouse clicked as Amanda paused the feed then backed it up to where the boy was lying in bed again. A few moments passed. *Click.*

1:36 a.m.—Subject sits up in bed.

Amanda's pulse began to beat against her neck forcefully. Cold sweat started to bead on her upper lip. She licked it clean and started the recording once more. The boy sat like that for what seemed like hours to Amanda. She stared at the screen, unable to avert her eyes. The boy stirred. *Click.*

1:39 a.m.—Subject stands and walks to the middle of the room.

Amanda licked her dry lips. Her throat suddenly felt tight and hot. She let out a quiet croak.

"What's that, Mandy?" Jerry asked but didn't look over from his desk. Amanda's hands trembled, and a shaky finger clicked once more.

She watched with horrified fascination as the boy just stood there, staring at the wall.

Suddenly, and she knew what was coming next, the boy cocked his head. *Click.*

1:41 a.m.—Subject moves to the wall opposite the bed and…presses ear against it.

There was nothing for Amanda to do but press on. She fumbled with the play button, clicking around it twice before successfully advancing the video. Her pulse smacked against her neck, thudding loudly in her ears. Shivering gooseflesh spread across her skin. No amount of licking would keep the small beads of cold sweat from her lip as it quivered. The liquid darkened her mask. Finally—*click.*

1:47 a.m.—Subject returns to bed.

Amanda stared at the monitor silently. The odd little boy, now balled up on the bed, was neatly tucked under the blankets with a thumb in his mouth. "There's no way," Amanda said finally with a rush of exhaled air.

"What?"

This time Jerry looked over. Concern wracked his face as he did. Amanda was as pale as snow and shivering like she was sitting in a pile of it. "Mandy?"

Jerry got up so fast his chair wheeled back into a filing cabinet, knocking over some recording equipment that rested on top. At once, he was beside her. He knelt and spun her chair so she was facing him.

For a moment, her eyes just stared into the nothingness above Jerry's head, her breath sharp and halted. The beads of cold sweat had joined together, making her skin gleam in the light of the monitor. "Mandy!?"

Jerry grabbed her by the shoulders and gave her a shake. It was like a scene from an old movie where the helpless female is catatonic and the strong male lead tries to bring her to her senses.

It was all he could think to do. It seemed to work.

Amanda's far-off eyes blinked once, then again. Then she focused and allowed them to fall and meet Jerry's concerned gaze.

"Jerry," she said, grabbing his sweater with both hands. Jerry's eyes grew wild with fear and surprise.

"What!? What, I'm here, what!?" he almost screamed, right in her face.

She blinked again and spoke calmly, "Call Dr. Luu."

CHAPTER 25

SAMANTHA WAS SNORING QUIETLY ON THE COUCH beside Jason as he surfed aimlessly through the tv channels, unable to find anything that would hold his attention. Distract him, in fact. He was starting to doze, though, eyes heavy from lack of sleep and the morning's stress.

Someone won a trip to Hawaii on *The Price Is Right.* Who the hell was traveling right now anyway? Jason thought. Stupid bastards, spreading COVID around like it's no big deal. How many people were dead in the U.S. now? A hundred thousand? Maybe a hundred and fifty? That's a lot of dead people in a few short months. This thing was serious, regardless of what the tin hat wearing conspiracy theorists said. He flipped over to an infomercial selling exercise equipment. The all-in-one machine that can fit in any home gym could do it all, apparently. The buff spokesperson and his sexy, scantily clad assistant demonstrated how easy the equipment was to use and pay for in three easy payments.

Jason frowned and absentmindedly grabbed at his belly fat as he contemplated his physical fitness.

No room for a home gym here, he thought. But I really do need to start working out again. Tomorrow maybe. I'll get up early and at least do some bodyweight stuff, maybe go for a run at lunch.

He had never been this lazy in his life. Tired and lethargic, constantly sapped of all energy.

Gravity pulled at his weak eyelids as he stared at the television. Some cooking show was on now with a portly older woman talking to the camera—something about selecting the perfect victim.

What? No, that couldn't be right.

The perfect cut of meat, she said.

Jason's head dipped slowly as sleep threatened to come. He blinked and muted the tv; this lady was talking crazy.

The camera now focused in on the woman's hands as she handled a large shoulder of beef. She flipped the thick, red muscle over in her hands, poking it and massaging oil into the flesh. The oil intensified the color of the meat into deep crimson, and the shoulder glistened in the studio lights.

Jason's stomach turned and a queasy feeling brewed in his guts. Still, he watched on.

In the muted silence, behind the snoring beside him and the traffic sounds far away, was a familiar sound, teasing his eardrums, pulsing against his brain. The hum throbbed in his temples as he watched Chef Portly Pants addressing the camera once again. Her once pristine white chef coat was now a mess of dark blood around her thick midsection. The large butcher's knife in her right hand was coated with pieces of flesh and dripped crimson. The camera zoomed in slowly, closing in on her round face. Her teeth were bared and savage, her light-blue eyes crazed and bloodshot. What was she saying?

Jason's dazed eyes followed her mouth as it moved, the hum pulsing behind the walls and in his mind. *Wah wah, wah wah.*

Her mouth was now following the slow pulse of the hum. *Muh wah, muh wah.*

Jason's eyes slowly blinked as he relaxed into the coming sleep.

"Muh wah," she said, in perfect time with the hum. Her eyes were intense and unchanging, staring at Jason. Her jaw opened and closed, and somehow her shrill and raspy voice now merged with the hum in sickening harmony, distantly screaming, "Mur dah! mur der!"

Finally Jason's eyes closed and his body went limp as he tumbled into the dark abyss of a fitful slumber.

* * *

Samantha's eyes flew open to the sound of rapid clacking as her phone vibrated against the wooden tabletop. She grabbed it quickly in a half daze. It was her mom. Samantha looked at the screen longingly, craving to talk with her mother; to hear the familiar sound of home. But she let the call go to voicemail. She listened quietly, hearing only the sounds of their apartment. Jason's steady, quiet breaths as he slept sitting up, his head tilted back against the cushion of the couch at an uncomfortable-looking angle, the tv remote gripped loosely in his hand.

Behind that was another familiar sound.

Something unrelenting. Incessant.

The canvas upon which all other sounds were painted. The hum.

Samantha's eyes moved from the peaceful-looking Jason to her phone, which notified her of a new voicemail. She needed to talk to her parents; she needed to hear their voices and feel their love. She wanted to tell them about the baby but thought that maybe she wouldn't. She couldn't bring herself to do it right now anyway. It was still all too fresh. And even though Samantha knew that miscarriage wasn't a rare occurrence, it felt surreal and not something she wanted to talk about—at least not yet.

And it may not even have been a miscarriage, Samantha thought. We won't know for sure until the tests come back.

Samantha looked up at the tv and wondered why the cooking show was muted. Jason twitched in his sleep. Samantha turned her head to see a look of what seemed like pain flash across his face and disappear. Samantha lay for a moment longer, propped up on her elbow. Jason stirred again. He flinched. Samantha sat up, facing Jason and clutching her arms to her chest. Jason grunted and twitched.

"Mmph."

The remote control slipped from his hand and landed on the floor with a smash, sending the two batteries from inside flying in separate directions. Samantha could only watch with frightened eyes. "Mm uh," he muttered, his voice like a pained moan. Sam's eyes welled with liquid, and her jaw clenched with a squeak of her teeth.

"Muh wah! Muh wah!"

Jason's voice built to a fever pitch, his eyes closed tight under his sweaty brow.

"Mur dah!"

Samantha didn't know what else to do, so she pressed her feet against his side and shook him. Gently at first, but then with more and more force until Jason's eyes flew open and his limp body became rigid and aware. He sat straight up, breathing heavily and clutching his chest. He wiped the sweat from his forehead and looked over at Sam. She looked like a beaten puppy, making herself as small as possible on the couch. Her face was scrunched, her eyes wide with fear.

"Babe?" Jason asked.

Samantha just continued to stare at him with that look of terror.

"What happened?"

Jason extended his arm towards her. She pulled back slightly at first but relented as she looked into his eyes. Samantha saw her man there, looking just as scared as she was. She bolted towards him and wrapped her arms around his neck.

"Oh, Jesus Jay!" she cried as the pools in her eyes finally breached the dam. "You were having a crazy dream, I guess. Convulsing and saying something...I don't know what, but it was so scary, Jay. Terrifying!"

Jason held her tight as she soaked his shoulder with her tears.

"I'm sorry, Sam," was all he could muster. "I'm so, so sorry."

After a while, Samantha and Jason finally peeled themselves apart. They looked at each other with knowing looks.

Jason broke the silence: "We look rough."

Samantha wiped at her face and nodded. "I'm going to shower. Will you come?"

"Of course."

They got up and went to the bathroom. Samantha turned on the shower and it whooshed to life. Without any words, the couple disrobed and hopped in under the water that hissed and eventually steamed up the room.

It was a small shower, so they had to take turns soaking,

then lathering, then rinsing. The hot water calmed Samantha, and she began to relax. Jason took the pink loofah from her hands and gently soaped her back. He finished, and she turned around.

"I love you," she said as she looked deep into his dark-blue eyes. Jason's mouth twitched into a smile as he lifted his hands to cup her face.

"I love you too," he whispered and kissed her quivering lips. As they kissed, Jason's phone lit up silently on the counter.

* * *

"Dr. Luu's office called," Jason said as they toweled off the remnants of their shower.

"Oh?" Samantha replied.

Jason dialed his voicemail and set it to speakerphone. Dr. Luu's voice asked Jason if he could make it in the next day. Jason looked at Sam with a worried frown on his face.

"He wants me to come in a day early," Jason said. "That can't be good."

He ended the voicemail and hung his towel on the rack.

"Maybe it's good news," Samantha offered. "Maybe he knows what's going on now and can help. He wants to help quicker than Wednesday."

"Maybe," Jason said unconvincingly.

The rest of the night, Jason couldn't stop running scenarios over in his mind. Why had the doctor called so late? What was so urgent that he wanted to move the appointment up? Jason worried while his mind played different clips of him standing in Dr. Luu's office, being told horrible, life-changing news. Cancer, a tumor, deep-seated psychological issues that would take a whole team of quacks to shrink his head down to nothing.

Samantha had fallen into a deep sleep almost immediately after her head hit the pillow, completely drained from the intense day. Jason tossed and turned for most of the night, unable to shut his mind off. When sleep finally did come, it was fitful and provided little rest.

CHAPTER 26

THE ALARM WAS CALLING OUT FROM INSIDE JASON'S end table. He cursed and pulled open the drawer, grabbed the phone, hit snooze, and rolled over with it still in his hand. He didn't bother pulling out any of the other things in the drawer to put them back where they were before he went to sleep; he just left the drawer hanging open.

The alarm crowed again, and Jason fought the urge to throw the phone at the wall. He sat up and rubbed his eyes. He was alone. Samantha was already up and in the other room. With no enthusiasm, Jason got out of bed, pulled on some clothes, and left the bedroom.

Samantha was stretched out on her yoga mat, her face aglow with perspiration.

"Morning," Jason said as he walked into the kitchen.
"Morning," Sam replied, a little breathlessly.

Jason grabbed a cup of coffee from the pot and added some cream from the fridge. The smell pulled at his senses, sharpening his focus as his brain prepared for caffeine. He watched Sam for a moment, jealous of her energy. He took a sip of the bitter liquid, headed into his office, and closed the door.

Sam looked up when she heard the familiar click and stared after him. Her phone came to life beside her, vibrating on the floor. When she answered, it was her doctor's office, asking if she could come in that afternoon.

I guess we'll both be getting bad news today, she thought and rested her glistening body down into child's pose.

Later, Samantha was sitting at the kitchen island, a plate with half a sandwich in front of her. She heard the keyboard cease its clicking, and soon Jason opened the door to the office.

"Hey," he said meekly.

"Hey," Sam replied. "How's it going in there?"

"Productive," he said. "But I'm so tired. I don't think I slept at all last night."

On another plate next to Sam was a sandwich stuffed with turkey and cheese. A dark-green pickle lay beside it.

"That's the last of the sandwich meat and bread," Sam said.

"That's ok; we can get some stuff tonight after I get home if you want."

Jason sat down and grabbed the hefty sandwich in both hands.

"Sure." Sam thought a moment. "I have an appointment this afternoon too."

Jason's sandwich stopped mid-air.

"The same time as my appointment?"

"Basically, yeah."

"Shit," Jason said. "I wanted to be there for that, for you. Will you be ok? I could reschedule…"

"No," Samantha interrupted. "It's ok, I'll be fine. We need to know what your doctor says too."

Jason finished his meal quickly, thanked Sam, and gave her a peck on the cheek.

"I have a bunch of stuff to do before I take off later, so I'm gonna head back to work, ok?"

Jason got up and rested his hand on Sam's shoulder. She put down her fork, clasped his hand in hers, and gave it a little squeeze.

"Ok."

At 3:30 p.m., Jason emerged from the office again. Samantha was focused on a sudoku puzzle on the couch. He brushed his teeth, showered, and got dressed. When he came back out into the living room, Samantha was putting on her shoes.

"Want me to drop you off?" Jason asked as he headed towards the apartment door.

"No, that's ok. I'd like a walk. It's only a few blocks anyway."

Jason slid on his shoes and jacket, and the couple headed out the door. The elevator dinged, and the door opened to the lobby. Samantha leaned in and gave Jason a quick kiss.

"Good luck," she whispered.

"You too, babe."

Jason watched her walk away as the chrome door closed, and he descended to the parking level.

* * *

After parking at the clinic, Jason checked his phone. Samantha hadn't texted. It hasn't been that long, he thought; she probably hasn't seen the doctor yet. Jason put his phone in his pocket, slipped on his surgical mask, and headed into the sleep clinic.

A few people were waiting in the plastic chairs in the

waiting room, but the receptionist took Jason back to Dr. Luu's office immediately.

"Hello, Jason!" Dr. Luu exclaimed from behind his desk. The receptionist smiled and left Jason standing in the doorway. He hesitated.

"Well? Come on in." Dr. Luu stood up and gestured to the chair in front of his desk.

"Hey, doc," Jason said as he entered the room and dropped himself down into a chair. He looked up at the doctor, completely stiff and on edge.

"How bad is it?" he asked.

Dr. Luu observed Jason carefully for a moment, hands clasped on the desk in front of him.

"Honestly Jason, it's not that bad."

Jason exhaled a breath that he had been holding since the doctor had called the night before. He relaxed back into the chair and risked a smile.

"Really." A statement instead of a question.

"The brain scan data was fairly normal except for a few blips."

"A few blips?" Jason asked, the now reinvigorated worry scratching at his throat.

"Nothing to be too concerned about, Jason. There was some talking, and you did sleepwalk."

Jason's face flushed with embarrassment. The thought of that creepy male nurse watching him talking and walking around all night sat uncomfortably in his chest.

"This is good, Jason," Dr. Luu said, noticing the discomfort on Jason's face. "Because now we have some good data from when you were having an occurrence."

Just call it what it is, doc, a fucking weirdo episode, Jason thought.

"Ok? So you haven't actually figured out why this is happening? Why am I here, doc?" Jason couldn't help the strained, annoyed tone of his voice. "Shouldn't you be working on it right now?" His face turned into a mean scowl.

Dr. Luu continued, unphased by Jason's change in demeanor.

"Please relax, Jason. I understand your frustration. Please understand we are working on the data, even at this very moment."

Jason did relax and felt that touch of flushed embarrassment again.

"Sorry, doc."

"It's ok; it happens all the time," Dr. Luu replied lightheartedly. "You're here because we need more data. I want to send you home with a portable monitor that you can wear when you sleep tonight. That should give us enough information to figure out what's going on and what we can do about it. How does that sound?"

Jason sat quietly for a moment.

"Well, I was hoping you had some answers today, and that's why you called, but I guess I'm happy that you believe there isn't anything serious going on. No tumors; no insanity."

"No, none of that, Jason. Physically, everything appears normal; I just need more data. And having the monitor on when you're in your natural…environment should provide all the information I need to help you."

"Sounds good, doc."

"Good, then here's the monitor. The instructions are in the box too. It's simple, but if you have any problems, call the number on the sheet, and someone will be able to assist."

Dr. Luu stood up and handed the small white box to Jason, who also got up.

"Thanks again, doc." Jason turned and left the office, disappointed but hopeful.

Dr. Luu sat back down in his office chair. He rubbed his chin thoughtfully with his thumb and forefinger. He clicked his mouse, and the monitor came to life, flooding his face with light. On the screen, two videos were paused—a man and a little boy standing against a wall, the same wall, listening to each other.

CHAPTER 27

JASON PARKED THE SUV AND ASCENDED IN THE elevator until it reached his floor. Inside the apartment, Samantha was hunched over her phone, sitting on the couch. Her dark hair was in a long braid that flowed down her white bathrobe. Jason kicked off his shoes, shrugged off his jacket, and walked into the living room with the white box in his hand. Samantha looked up at him and then down at the box.

"How did it go?" she asked as she put her phone down on the coffee table and straightened up.

"They need more data, I guess."

Jason sat down on the couch beside Samantha and placed the monitor on the coffee table in front of them.

"I gotta wear this stupid thing tonight," he said with a heavy sigh.

"Well, at least they're working on it. The doctor didn't say anything else at all?"

"He tried reassuring me that everything was pretty much normal, but I dunno if I fully believe him. He wasn't telling me everything. I know that for sure." "Well, he probably doesn't want to say anything until he has more information. I'm sure if he said things looked normal, then that's a good thing, Jay." "I guess," Jason said. "Not much I can do but wear the stupid monitor anyway."

The room was quickly darkening as the sun set behind the earth. Jason got up and turned on a few lights to inspect the contents of the white box.

Samantha stood up, gathered her fuzzy robe around herself, and headed to the kitchen to fix dinner. She was craving comfort food; some good ol' home cookin'.

She popped open the fridge and frowned. They were going to need groceries soon, but there was enough here for dinner. She pulled out two fat chicken breasts and a bag of carrots and set them on the island. She opened a door under the island and grabbed two handfuls of mini potatoes. Meat and potatoes might just be the best comfort food there is, she thought.

The kitchen soon came alive with the sounds of washing and cutting and frying and boiling. Samantha moved gracefully between tasks, a blur of white cotton as she chopped the carrots and checked on the meat.

The complex smell of rosemary mixed with garlic hit Jason's nostrils like a truck, setting his mouth to water. He inhaled deeply in his seat at the island.

"Gooooddamn, that smells good," he said with a smile, his dimples popping from under his beard. Samantha looked up from her carrots and smiled back; the earlier tension of the day seemed to have floated away on the scent of seared chicken and herbs.

Jason found himself grateful she wasn't cooking steak but couldn't find the reason why.

He smiled again. "We should go for a walk tonight; looks like it's going to be a nice one."

"Yeah?" Sam replied and looked out the window. The sun had disappeared behind the horizon, and fierce color marked the clear, early evening sky. "Sounds like a plan," she said as her eyes went back to her work.

"Sure you don't need a hand?"

"Too many cooks in the kitchen, Jay."

* * *

After dinner and after Jason had finished the dishes, the couple put on their shoes and jackets and left the apartment. With a few dings of the elevator, they were in the lobby. Chester was sitting behind the concierge desk with his nose buried deep in a book. "Evening, Chester," Jason said with a hidden smile.

"Good evening, you two. How are you tonight?" "Not too bad," Jason said as he and Samantha slowed their pace. "You're the concierge tonight?"

"Good help is hard to find," Chester replied with a light-hearted sigh. "The new guy was a no-show, so I gotta pick up the slack."

Chester's eyes squinted from his masked smile and he added, "I don't mind, though. It lets me catch up on my reading."

Chester pointed at his book.

Jason chuckled and Samantha smiled as they continued to the lobby door.

"Fair enough, sir," Jason said. "We'll see you later." Chester nodded and went back to his book as the couple left the lobby and stepped onto the sidewalk.

The night was cool, but not offensively so. The air blowing in from the harbor filled their lungs with fragrant ocean mist and the smell of salt and fish. They walked down towards the seawall, close to where the collision with the cyclist had occurred. Jason rubbed his shoulder at the thought.

Other people were also walking along the seawall, enjoying the calm night. Mostly other couples, holding hands as they quietly strolled beside the ocean. The dark water lapped lazily against the manmade shore. There were no waves, no surf, but the water still moved against the rocks and around the barnacle-covered wooden piers and white, fiberglass boats as if it were alive.

It was alive after all, wasn't it? The ocean teemed with life: a vast ecosystem of flora and fauna, so diverse and different yet depending on each other for survival. The ocean itself took on the properties of a living being, didn't it? Breathing its tides in and out as it was pushed and pulled by the moon. The ocean was called a body of water for a reason.

"I want to go home."

The words brought Jason out of his lull. The way the pure white boats floated on the black water was hypnotizing. The occasional gull cried out as it made its way to its evening resting place. Heat flared in Jason's guts.

"We already went over this," he said dismissively. Sam stopped and leaned against the railing, looking out into the harbor. Jason slowed, and then turned and joined in beside her.

"We…" he began.

"I don't mean today," she interrupted, "it doesn't have to be today. But I want to go home, Jason."

She used his full name, which meant she was as serious as the cold, hard look in her eyes. He knew he wasn't going to be able to fight this one. And why would he? he thought. Did he really like it out here anyway? What was so great about

Seattle? His brain went over some scenarios where the pandemic never happened. Would have been happy then? The fire in his belly cooled, and his shoulders relaxed.

"The pandemic can't last forever, babe," he said, looking out to the water. "And we need to get the results of this sleep test; maybe this doctor can help. Maybe he can figure out what's wrong and fix it, or help me fix it. You have to give me that much."

His voice had turned indignant and demanding, the liquid fire boiling up again inside. "And we can get a new place, somewhere bigger, without that fucking hum."

There was a finality in his voice that Samantha didn't like. Her brow furrowed, and her expression only hardened.

"Obviously, I want you to get better, Jay. But I need to take care of my health too," she said.

Jason flashed a look over at Samantha's stern face. Guilt raced up his spine and rested heavily in his mind. He realized he hadn't even asked her how she was. How her appointment had gone. He had been too wrapped up in his own shit; too worried about the sleep disturbances and the hum

(Francine probably did need cleaning, though)

to consider Sam's feelings. But why not? She looked fine, really. And they could always make another baby.

But damnit, he was going crazy over here! Literally out of his goddamn gourd! Maybe she was the selfish one, after all, demanding to go home right in the middle of him working on getting better. Maybe—

Jason's thoughts were interrupted as Samantha turned and began walking again, towards the little market a few blocks away.

"I'm not saying we need to leave today or tomorrow. We will see what the doctor says and go from there."

The couple walked to the market in silence. Once inside, Samantha and Jason grabbed a few essentials from the shelves: meat and cheese, eggs, and milk. They paid at the register, grabbed their bags, and headed out the door, sanitizing their hands along the way.

Samantha and Jason turned up the street with fists full of bags and headed for their apartment. Only a few words had passed between them since their talk, and they were both eager to get inside and go to bed early, putting another dreadful day in the past.

Jason opened the large lobby door for Samantha, and they entered the building. Their shoes clicked against the lobby floor as they passed Chester's office. The light was on and the door open. The couple looked in as they passed to see Chester sitting at his desk, completely engulfed in his book. Jason pushed the round up-arrow button on the wall, and it lit up. He took a step back and looked up to the small LED screen above the elevators. One was coming down from PH, and the other was coming up from P2. Samantha and Jason shuffled themselves in front of the elevator from parking level two, since it would be there first. With a ding, the doors opened. Jason dropped his bags, and the meat and milk smacked the hard floor with a clap inside ruffled plastic. Samantha jumped at the sound and turned to look at Jason. His eyes were wide and transfixed on the open elevator.

"Jay?" She looked from Jason to the elevator and back. "Jason, what's wrong?"

"Do you see?" he asked meekly.

"See what?"

"Do you see them?"

Samantha looked into the elevator and back at Jason.

"Jason, you're scaring them; what's wrong?"

The elevator dinged. Samantha thrust her foot in front of the closing door, and it popped back open hesitantly.

"I'm so sorry," she said to the occupants. "Do you mind if we ride with you?"

Jason blinked with realization. She *does* see them.

"Jason," Sam hissed. "Let's go."

Jason quickly picked up the fallen bags and headed into the elevator to stand beside a very annoyed-looking middle-aged woman and a very strange-looking little boy.

Another ding and the elevator door began to close. Samantha reached for the panel to press the button for their floor, paused halfway, and then let her arm drop. Jason, who was staring straight ahead, frozen, looked down at the panel and saw what Sam had seen. Their floor button was already lit. Jason's eyes squinted as his mind raced. He couldn't remember ever seeing anyone else from their floor, which was not uncommon in a large apartment building. Even more common now that people were staying home for the majority of their day. Jason could feel the little boy's piercing eyes looking up at him, cold and unblinking.

Jason watched the little boy in his peripherals. He was holding the hand of who Jason could only assume was his mother. Jason cleared his throat and stole a glance down at the boy. The kid gave Jason the creeps, no doubt about that. Jason's eyes moved from the boy's shined, tiny black shoes up the brown tweed pants that disappeared under his tiny light-brown trench coat.

Jason couldn't help but take in the sight of the boy. What

child dressed like this? Maybe it was his mother who had put the outfit together. A thought flashed into Jason's mind. Had she noticed him checking out the kid? Jason didn't think so. If she had, she'd think Jason was some sicko looking to get pervy, and she would grab her child close to protect him.

Jason continued his inspection as the child continued to stare. Finally, past the boy's thin, colorless lips and white porcelain cheeks, Jason's tired eyes met a familiar sight.

The boy's eyes revealed the exhaustion that his hard face attempted to conceal. The dark skin around his eyes was in stark contrast to his white cheeks. It almost looked as if the child was wearing makeup to black out the bags under his tired eyes. Jason and the boy stood in hidden conversation with their eyes locked until the mother finally noticed and pulled her son close, an arm around his chest.

Jason looked back at the elevator door. The bell sounded as they slowed to a stop. The door opened, and Samantha and Jason exited and headed to their apartment. The mother and son followed, not far behind.

Samantha pulled out her keys and slid one in the lock. With a click and a turn of the knob, the apartment door opened. Samantha entered and Jason followed, but he stopped in the doorway and looked back. The boy was still staring at Jason, peering out from behind his mother's legs. The woman released her lock and opened their door.

"Guh…Goodnight." Jason's sudden and awkward voice startled the woman. She regained composure quickly and nodded back. She pushed the boy firmly into her apartment and disappeared behind him, shutting the door and locking it with a click.

Inside the apartment, Samantha kicked off her shoes and

put her bags down on the kitchen floor. She grabbed the antiseptic wipes and began wiping down their groceries. Jason stood staring at the door for a moment, then finally kicked off his shoes too. He joined Samantha in the kitchen and set his bags down beside hers.

"Good thing the eggs were in my bags," she jabbed as she continued sanitizing the groceries. Jason joined in, still in a half daze, thinking everything over.

"Well? What the hell was that down there?" Samantha asked, tired of waiting for Jason to speak. Jason continued putting away sterile packages, but Sam had stopped wiping things. She was leaning against the stove, her arms crossed in front of her.

"It's crazy," he finally said.

"Try me," Sam replied.

"I've seen them before."

"Duh, Jay, they're our neighbors."

"No, not here." He paused.

Samantha's thin patience was palpable.

"Where, Jason?"

"At the clinic."

CHAPTER 28

SAMANTHA BREWED SOME CHAMOMILE TEA AND SET down a mug for each of them on the coffee table. She sat down beside Jason, who was staring past the dark television, out the window, and into the night sky. "This is a good thing," Samantha finally said.

Jason turned to look at her, then grabbed his steaming mug and brought it to his lips. He tried a sip, but the hot liquid burned his lips, so he put the drink back down.

"It's creepy as hell; that's what it is."

Jason looked back out the window sullenly.

"What are the chances?"

"Uh, I'd say pretty good, Jay. Considering you both are having sleeping problems, and you both live on the same floor in the same building." Samantha paused. "Jason, we share walls with those people." Samantha quickly quieted at this thought, remembering the times she found Jason pressed up against the wall, listening—a wall they shared with the strange little boy and his mother.

"Maybe the sound in the walls is messing with that little boy too, Jay."

Jason continued to stare.

"We should go ask them if they hear it. If it bothers them too."

Jason looked over at Sam with malice in his eyes.

"Are you dumb?"

Samantha recoiled.

"I'm not going over there asking about some sound in the walls, Sam. Of course they hear it; it's loud as shit and never shuts. The fuck. UP!"

Jason leapt up and headed to one of the walls they shared with the apartment next door. He could feel the hum behind the paint and drywall. He pressed his fingertips against the flat surface and closed his eyes.

The vibration danced along his fingers, up his arms, and into his head. His jaw clenched and he ground his teeth. His face flushed and a single bead of sweat formed on his temple before dropping down the side of his face, leaving a salty trail.

Samantha watched him from the couch, then finally got up and went to Jason, putting her hand on his back.

"Jason," she said calmly, "It's a good thing because it means there is something wrong with this place, not with you."

Jason shrugged her hand away and turned around. "If you want to leave so damn bad, just go." His words were thick acid escaping from his mouth. Samantha stared into Jason's eyes with her mouth open in stunned surprise. He stared back coldly, his eyes an angry blue ocean.

"Well?" he asked, unfazed by her hurt expression. "You've hated it since we got here. You haven't even given it a chance!" Jason's voice picked up volume. Samantha could only stare, barely recognizing the man in front of her.

"Wha—" Samantha began.

"Wha, wha, wha," Jason interjected. "Wha, wha, whining bitch! That's all you do. Fucking whine about everything instead of getting up and doing something. Your stupid puzzles and dumbass knitting. The fuck."

Jason's voice became harsher and harsher, his breathing labored. His eyes were wide and accusatory. Samantha's face flushed and her eyes welled over.

"What the fuck Jason!?" she screamed.

Jason flinched in surprise. Samantha very rarely swore or raised her voice, but her rage only spurred Jason on.

He continued, "I have this great opportunity out here. I could be running this goddamn company one day! You don't give a shit about that. Like you want me to fail? You want me to be a big fuck-up failure. That's it, huh?"

"How dare you!" Samantha shot back. "I haven't been there for you? Everything is about you, Jason! It's always about your job, your opportunity, your office," she continued, her voice ramping up. "It's your fucked-up sleeping shit, Jason. That's the reason everything is so fucked! I've been here, supporting you, trying to help. But you're fucking losing it, Jay!"

"Well! Sorry I have bullshit sleeping problems, Sam. It's not like I asked for it! I didn't ask God one day to fuck my sleep all up so I'd go fucking crazy! Jesus Christ, Sam. You're so selfish!"

Samantha's eyes widened and her face turned fierce. "Are you kidding me, Jason?" she hissed. "You must be kidding me. I'm in a mental institution right now."

"What!?" Jason said indignantly.

Samantha paused to take a deep, shuddering breath. "You didn't even ask me how MY appointment went, Jason. You didn't even ask about the baby." Jason's eyes dropped to the floor. "That's because it's all about you, Jay. But you're so self-involved you don't even see how selfish you really are."

There was a finality to her voice. Jason stood staring at the floor, his hands shaking and his lips trembling.

"It doesn't matter."

"What? What doesn't matter?"

Jason's trembling voice found strength and resolve. "We can make another goddamn baby Sam! But I'm losing my mind here. I can't get that back. Miscarriage of the fucking brain, Sam!"

The anger and fury drained from Samantha's face and was replaced by loathing and disgust.

"Fuck you, Jason," she said, and then turned towards the bedroom. "You son of a bitch."

Jason stared after her until she disappeared into the room, slamming the door behind her.

He paused a moment, letting the events settle, and then walked to the closed door. Behind it, he could hear Samantha's loud, fitful sobs. His mouth hardened into a thin line as her crying fueled his resentment and the burning fire in his belly.

Jason busted into the room to see Samantha sitting on the edge of the bed, facing away from the door. She jumped a little, startled by the loud noise, but didn't turn around. Jason stood and stared at her back, breathing heavily with his fists clenched. Finally, he went to the closet, grabbed a spare pillow and a thin blanket, and rushed back out the door, closing it hard behind himself. He stormed over to the couch, threw down the blanket and pillow, and turned off the apartment lights. He crawled under the blanket and stared straight up at the dark ceiling.

His anger was still bubbling, his heart still pumping heavy blood that made his temples throb. He looked down and over at the coffee table where the white box sat.

"Damnit," he said and sat up.

Jason grabbed the box and flipped open the top. He

pulled out the contents and used the flashlight on his cell-phone to read the instructions. It looked easy enough from the diagram, he thought.

He really just wanted to curl up and get some rest, but he needed the doctor to help. And the only way the doctor was going to help was with the data from this stupid machine.

Jason hung the small electronic box around his neck, where it rested on his solar plexus. He found the electrode heads and attached them to his face where the diagram instructed. Next, he plugged the wires into the box and flicked the switch.

A red and green LED bulb flashed slowly on the face of the box.

"Guess that's it."

Jason took in a deep breath and let it out slowly. He lay down and pulled the blanket up to his chest, staring at the ceiling again. The blood that pounded on his eardrums began to relent as he relaxed into his pillow. He closed his eyes, and as the deafening sound abated, it was replaced by the distant sounds of sobbing, and just behind that: the hum.

* * *

Samantha's hard, uncontrollable sobs began to diminish into soft, whimpering breaths. She sat on the edge of the bed as tears steadily rolled down her face. She sniffed and wiped at her hot, wet face with the sleeve of her robe. With a shuddering sigh she stood up and went to the bathroom. She grabbed a roll of toilet paper, making sure not to look at herself in the mirror, and headed back to her bed. Her breath came and went in a steadying rhythm, and her eyes began to dry. She wiped her face with a wad of toilet paper and blew her nose while staring out the window. The night sky was dark with thick clouds, and the ocean's surface rough from a north wind.

A few fat raindrops smacked against the glass at an unsettling, sporadic tempo.

Samantha lifted up her legs, deposited them beneath the blanket, and lay down. She picked up her phone from the nightstand and punched in her password. She stared at her conversation with her mother as the smacking of raindrops against the windows quickened. She wanted to ask for help. To tell them everything. But her fingers paused, unable to type.

What could they do? she wondered.

Nothing right now; they would just worry. Samantha shut the screen off, replaced the phone on the tabletop, and turned out the light. She would call tomorrow when she's had some rest.

Samantha lay back and listened to the hypnotic beating of the rain against the glass. Her tight muscles relaxed as the sound soothed her. Suddenly very aware of her exhaustion, Samantha's heavy eyes closed.

Then—something woke her up. Her eyes jerked open. How long had she been asleep? Had she even slept? The rain was still beating against the window. Her muscles tightened as she lay completely still, looking over at the door. A shape was standing in the doorway, strange red and green lights blinking madly on its chest. It just stood there, its shoulders heaving up and down, up and down. Time passed at a crawl as she watched the shadow watching her. Her heart quickened, and her hands and feet went numb, pricked by invisible needles. Samantha fought to keep her breath steady and calm, pretending to be asleep.

Finally, the figure twitched and began to move towards her. She shut her eyes. The couch is not good for sleeping, she thought. Jason is just coming to bed. The thought relaxed her some as she listened to Jason walk quietly across the floor to stand beside the bed. Samantha felt the weight of his body lie down beside her as she continued to focus on her breath.

Slow and steady. She didn't want him to know she was awake. She didn't want to talk. Not right now, anyway. She needed sleep to regain her strength and shake the clouds from her mind so she could talk some sense into Jason.

Samantha's thoughts were interrupted by Jason's touch. His hand brushed her arm as he shifted his weight. Samantha stiffened once more. Jason slowly flipped his leg over her hips, straddling her and then allowing his weight to settle onto her. Samantha froze, her mind racing.

He wants sex? she thought. Right now. That's what he's thinking about?

Her eyes opened in slits, just enough to see the dark body above her, the green and red lights blinking offensively. Her eyelids opened further as her sight adjusted to the darkness. Her focus went from the blinking box up his chest, past his heaving shoulders, to his face. Cold and blank. Just like his eyes. She was expecting him to be looking at her, but he wasn't. He was staring into the nothingness above her head. A single tear escaped her eye as hot panic boiled in her guts.

"Ja—"

At once, his hands were around her neck. Her eyes shot open in terror. His eyes were staring into hers now. Dark blue and menacing. Samantha pushed and struggled against his body. She grabbed at his wrists and tried to work them apart. But he only squeezed harder. A large vein pulsed in his forehead as his heart pumped thick, hot blood through his body.

"Please," Sam gasped, "Jason."

His lips curled upwards into a maniacal grin. Samantha grabbed at the grin, pushing against his face. He was too strong, and she was weakening—white spots flashed across her field of vision. In a final, desperate move, she dug her nails into the side of his face and pulled down as hard as she could. Jason screamed in pain. He released his grip on her neck and grabbed his own face, writhing in pain.

Samantha coughed and gasped for breath. Her throat cried out in agony as she gulped in precious lungsful of air.

"You bitch!" he screamed as he looked at the blood on his hands. Samantha felt a surge of powerful energy as she bucked Jason off her hips and onto the floor with a thud. She sprang up quickly and ran to the bathroom, closing and locking the door.

She rubbed her throat, red from trauma, and walked backward until her knees hit the toilet bowl. She sat down, not taking her eyes off the door. She could hear Jason cursing and moving around in the bedroom. Samantha jumped as he smashed something against the wall, something wooden. She thought of her nightstand. She thought of her phone that was left there. She was trapped, shaking, and alone.

BOOM, BOOM, BOOM against the door.

"I'm gonna kill you, you bitch!" Jason yelled from the other side.

BOOM! once more.

"You're dead!"

Suddenly the banging stopped, and she heard Jason move to the office. Samantha's blood turned to ice. Hyperventilating with tears streaming down her face, she looked hopelessly around the small bathroom for something, anything she could use as a weapon. She grabbed the toilet brush and held it up. "Fuck!" she yelled. "Help!!"

She jumped into the shower and slammed her fists against the wall.

"Please! Help me! Please!!"

Samantha banged again, so hard that one of her wrists cracked and sent an explosion of pain up to her head. She screamed in a mix of terror and agony.

She jumped out of the shower, opened the cupboards under the sink, and began throwing makeup and toiletries out with big sweeps of her arms until she saw it.

She grabbed the small but heavy pipe from under the sink.

BOOM! against the door again. Samantha jumped and fell back against the wall. The sound of something hitting the door. Wood on wood. Again.

CRACK!

The door split open just wide enough for the butt of a shotgun to come through. Jason pulled the stock from the door and bent over to look in. His eyes were crazed, and his maniacal grin only wider. Samantha shrieked at the sight of this man that looked nothing like her lover.

"Jason stop! Please Jay!" she cried.

His face disappeared from the hole.

"Oh I'll stop alright," he hissed. "As soon as I get my hands around that pretty little neck of yours again." Jason reached through the hole in the door and grabbed for the handle. Samantha lifted the pipe without pause and brought it down as hard as she could on Jason's grasping hand. The sound of pounded meat and cracking bone rang out in the bathroom.

"Aaarrghhh!" Jason screamed in painful anger. "Fuck! You fucking bitch!"

He slammed his good hand against the door. "Francine's gonna cut you in half!"

The brightly polished shotgun barrels appeared through the hole in the door. Samantha gasped and fell backward onto the floor, dropping the pipe with a clang.

"Are you fucking ready, bitch!?"

The shotgun bobbed around in the hole.

"Get ready to meet your fucking maker, you bi—" The silver barrel disappeared from the hole as Samantha heard a loud thud. She stared at the hole, her breath coming in sharp, frantic spurts that stabbed her throat like daggers.

She listened intently for any clue about what had happened, but all she could hear was her own breath and beating heart in her temples.

"Sam?" a voice finally broke through. "Samantha, are you in there? Are you ok?"

"Chester," she said dumbly. "Chester!?"

Feelings of relief washed over her as she began to sob. She made herself get up off the floor and opened the door, suddenly exhausted and acutely aware of every scratch and bruise.

"Sam," Chester said with apologetic eyes. Beneath him lay Jason, unconscious from the baseball bat in Chester's hand.

"Are you ok?" he asked, knowing that she, in fact, was not. Movement at the front door made Samantha look over. Their neighbors were standing there: the woman and the strange little boy. Samantha stared at them dumbly as the woman turned to usher the boy away. "Wait!" Samantha croaked.

The woman paused and looked back as Samantha half ran to the door. She stopped when she reached the woman. She grabbed on to the door frame in an effort to hold herself up as she wheezed and gasped for breath.

"Did you call Chester?"

The woman nodded.

Samantha took another labored breath.

"Did you call the police?"

The woman shook her head.

"Why not?"

Samantha's squinting, confused eyes followed the woman's gaze down to the long sleeves of her dark shirt. The woman pulled the material back to reveal her forearms, scarred with thin lines. There were fresh wounds also, Samantha observed, covered by reddening gauze. Samantha's shocked eyes looked back up at the woman's face.

"What happened? Who did this?"

The woman allowed her sleeves to drop once more as she reached a hand around the boy's shoulders.

"Him?"

The woman nodded.

"But why?"

"I don't know why." The woman's Irish accent was thick in Samantha's ears.

"Stuart is a fine young lad."

The boy looked up at the woman with tired, remorseful eyes.

"But something changed in him when we moved here. Just small, attitude issues at first—talking back and being moody. He wasn't sleeping well and started doing the strangest things at night. I woke up a few times to find him standing against the wall. Just standing there with his ear pressed up against it. At first I thought he was trying to eavesdrop on our neighbors, but when I called out to give him hell, I woke him up and he must have been confused and frightened, so he lashed out and got me pretty good." The woman gestured at her forearms.

"I took him to see the sleep doctor, hoping that we could fix his sleep, which would perhaps fix his other problems too."

The woman looked down at Stuart as she caressed his shaggy brown hair.

"But when the lift opened tonight and I saw the man from the sleep clinic looking so crazed and frightened, something clicked. And when you exited on the same floor as us, I knew. I knew it was not Stuart's fault. It was this place. There is something wrong with this place and it is ruining us!"

Samantha remembered Chester's story about the couple who had lived in the apartment before she and Jason. How they seemed so in love and ended up hating each other. She thought about the parallels between how Jason and the boy changed, slowly, when they moved in here. But what caused it? Samantha thought. Surely it had to be the hum, but how, and why? What the hell was it?

"Is he ok?"

Samantha's thoughts were broken by the woman's question. Sam looked back to where the woman was staring.

"Physically? I think so."

The weight of the situation suddenly struck Samantha and her eyes filled with liquid. She began to sob, staring at Jason's limp body. The woman placed a warm hand on Samantha's back and rubbed soothingly.

"You're going to be alright."

Samantha turned and threw herself into the arms of her neighbor, tears running down her cheeks.

"You'll be ok," the woman repeated softly. "But you need to get out."

The woman grabbed Samantha's shoulders and held her at arm's length.

"You must get out. Get him away from this wretched place. Leave as soon as you can, alright?" Samantha wiped her eyes and nodded. "Alright."

EPILOGUE

THE ROAD HOME

Samantha read the sign—Welcome to Idaho— as she drove past on the I-90 headed east. It would be a long drive home, but the further she got from Seattle and the apartment with the evil hum, the better she felt.

She put the window down a crack and breathed in the fresh mountain air. The road through Spokane Valley and the mountains was gorgeous. The sun shone brightly in the cloudless sky and looked like it would stay that way until they reached Missoula in a few hours.

Sam looked over at Jason. He was sleeping soundly in his seat, half reclined, a thin pillow under his head.

Initially she thought Chester had killed him the night before. Jason looked dead when she opened the broken bathroom door to see him lying in a heap, bleeding from his head. But shortly after speaking with the woman at the door, Jason had groaned and stirred on the floor. He grasped for his head and pulled himself up to a kneel. He pulled back a wet, warm hand and looked at the blood in confused horror.

"What happened?" he mumbled, wincing at the pain. Jason looked away from his crimson hand and saw Francine lying by the door. His dazed eyes looked up at the hole.

Realization dawned on his face as he looked up at Samantha, who was glaring at him, terrified and angry.

"What did I do!?" Jason gasped.

"You don't remember?" Chester asked as he eyed Jason with suspicion. Jason's eyes went from Sam to Chester and back to Sam.

"It's…foggy. I don't." His eyes dropped to the floor, and he began crying. Samantha knelt beside him and put her arm around his shuddering shoulders.

"What the fuck is wrong with me, Sam?" he cried. "Did I try to hurt you?"

He looked up and saw the red lines on Samantha's throat that were beginning to turn purple and swell. His eyes widened.

"Oh shit, Sam. Babe. Did I do that!?" he asked in shocked horror as he stared into her eyes. "I couldn't have, no way, I…"

"It's ok," she whispered. "It wasn't you, Jay, not really."

He continued to weep as his tears mingled with the dark blood, now beginning to clot where Samantha had scratched him.

"This place is evil, Jay. We have to get out. Now."

Her voice was calm and firm, but Jason needed no convincing.

"Can we leave right now?" he asked meekly.

"Soon, sweety," she cooed. "Let's get you cleaned up first."

Samantha grabbed the paper cup from the middle console and took a long drink. She put it back down and allowed herself to feel a small pang of guilt. She shouldn't be drinking caffeine, but there were a couple hundred more miles to drive, and she felt like she hadn't slept in days. Sometimes you gotta do what you gotta do to survive. Her thoughts shifted back to the night before as she zoned out on the road ahead.

Chester had helped her move a busted and bloodied Jason from the floor to the bathroom. Jason sat dazed on the toilet while they cleaned his wounds with alcohol and bandaged him up the best they could.

"Those lines will scar," Chester said as he inspected their work.

"I had to."

"I know." Chester shot Samantha a sympathetic look. Samantha turned on the faucet and ran a washcloth underneath the running water until it darkened and soaked up as much cool water as it could. She turned the tap off, wrung the cloth out, and dabbed at her face.

What a scene, she thought. She looked broken and tired. Beat-up and bruised. Chester watched her with pity in his eyes. Jason sat hunched over, looking like he had just lost a barroom brawl. She looked at the door and back at Chester.

"We have to leave."

"I know," he said.

"We'll pay to fix what we broke, obviously. And whatever the cost to get out of the lease early."

She finished wiping off her face and neck, put the facecloth down, and opened a drawer.

"I'll let you out of the lease, Sam. Don't worry about that." Chester watched as Samantha pulled out a bottle of aspirin and popped three in her mouth. She handed three to Jason as well, then took a long drink from the tap. She turned around to face the big man who had saved her life.

"I don't know what I'd have done if you didn't come,

Chester." She wrapped her arms around him as best she could and squeezed. Chester was taken aback briefly but softened into her embrace and patted her back gently.

"Thank you."

"You should thank Mrs. Sweeny next door. And her boy Stuart. They heard you through the walls and called down in a panic."

Samantha let Chester go and dropped her arms. "They said it sounded like someone was in trouble up here, and I should hurry."

"Glad you did," Sam said as she rubbed her neck. Then she said, "What about our stuff?"

"Well," Chester said and rubbed his chin, "take what you can, the essentials, I guess, and we can arrange for someone to come in and pack everything else up and ship it out to you. Thankfully, you didn't bring much to begin with."

Samantha sighed.

"Thank you, Chester. Thanks for everything."

The mountains had shrunk and smoothed out into rolling hills as they traveled east. Samantha pulled the black SUV into the hotel parking lot. Her body ached and cried for sleep. Jason stirred and sat up in his seat, taking in the scenery around them. Sam rolled to a stop in front of the hotel's big sliding doors and put the vehicle in park.

"I'll just be a minute," she said and turned off the engine. As she grabbed the door handle, Jason's hand touched her forearm, and she paused.

"Thank you, Sam," he said in a hushed voice.

She looked back at Jason, and a small but warm smile appeared on her face.

"It's going to be ok, Jay. I love you."

He smiled back. Samantha covered her smile with a light-blue surgical mask and headed into the hotel lobby.

A short while later, Samantha reappeared from behind the sliding doors with the small white envelope in her hands that held the room keys. She hopped back up into the seat and fired up the engine. She found a parking space, and they both got out of the car. Jason commented that the sun felt amazing as he grabbed his large duffle bag from the back seat. Samantha paused and closed her eyes, angling her face up to the sun. She basked in its warmth for a moment longer and then retrieved her own bag from the SUV. They headed towards the hotel again, and Samantha used the key pass to unlock the door. The green light lit up, announcing access was granted, and they entered and started looking for their room. It happened to be right beside the door, so Samantha held her pass up to the keypad once more.

It beeped red.

No entry.

She tried again. This time the light blinked green, and the mechanism moved the lock back so they could enter.

Samantha dropped her heavy bag onto the dark-green chair that sat in the corner of the room. Jason came in after her and set his duffle down on the floor. The door closed behind him with a click. Samantha walked back past the tv and the king-sized bed and into the bathroom. She relieved herself and then washed her hands thoroughly, making a point to not look at herself in the mirror. Samantha didn't care to see herself rugged and disheveled from the long night and long drive. She didn't want to see the progression of the bruises on her neck. She guessed they didn't look great, judging by the looks she had gotten from the front desk staff. She didn't care what they thought, though. She only cared about rest. And then to get home.

She thought about calling or texting her mother while she changed into more comfy clothes. She definitely needed some sleep before she made that call, she thought and jumped up on the bed. She could hear the shower running in the bathroom. Hot steam billowed from it and disappeared into the bedroom air. Samantha lifted the covers back and buried herself underneath. She thought briefly about turning on the tv but saw that the remote was far away, on the table across the room. Her eyes drifted down, and she wondered if there was anything in the little fridge, suddenly very aware of her thirst.

They would go grab some food later, she thought, after a quick nap.

She settled into the bed, and her head sank into the soft, fluffy down of the hotel pillow. Her muscles softened and relaxed into the mattress as she worked to keep the thoughts and memories of the past day out of her mind. Her eyes finally closed, and she began to nod off, faintly aware that the shower had been turned off. She heard the drips from the showerhead as it expelled the last of the water.

She heard Jason toweling off and slowly opened her eyes to see him inspecting himself in the mirror, tracing his fingers down the scarlet lines on his face. Her eyes closed once more, and she heard the click of the bathroom light.

Quiet now.

Peace and quiet.

A few more drips hit the shower floor.

Jason's breath, in and out, as he stood, naked in the center of the room.

But there was something behind his breath, behind the sound of the water dripping from the showerhead. Something familiar. Something humming. Samantha's eyes flew open with recognition and terror.

How!? she thought with despair. How did it find us!? How is this possible!? She saw a flash of movement in her peripheral and gritted her teeth, expecting the inevitable.

Visions of Jason on top of her, finishing what he had started, flashed across her mind. She was frozen in place. She couldn't move. Maybe she didn't really want to move. It would be easier to just let it happen.

But the baby!

This last thought made her bolt upright in the huge bed and let out a loud "No!" as she looked over to where Jason was kneeling in the corner. This made him jump, and Samantha heard a loud *thump!* Confused, she grabbed for the switch on the lamp, found it, and pulled hard, nearly taking the thing apart. She gasped for air, rubbing her throat and staring at the corner where Jason sat, rubbing his head with one hand and holding the refrigerator cord in the other. He looked up at her, puzzled, then back at the cord in his hand, understanding immediately.

With guilty eyes and a morose look upon his face, he said, "It was just the fridge, babe."

THE END

AUTHOR'S NOTE

Thank you, reader. I truly hope you enjoyed reading this novel. It is my first. My baby, and I am so happy to see it out in the world!

Please visit danhawleywrites.com and sign up for my non-spammy newsletter and follow me @danhawleywrites on Instagram and Facebook so we can connect! There are many more books in the works!

I would also humbly ask that you head over to Amazon and leave me an honest review or rating. It really helps indie authors like me develop and grow as creatives!

With appreciation,

DH

16147547R00140